*Peter shuddered.
"It's cold up here.
And I can't see anything
with all this fog."*

I spun Peter around. "There," I whispered hoarsely. "See them?"

"I sure do," Peter said, suddenly wide awake. The fog separated and we watched as four shadowy figures drifted into a fenced-in area. And then, without warning, they were gone. It was as if the air had swallowed them up without a trace. And then the fog closed in again and we couldn't even see the gate.

Peter and I just stared at each other. "Wh-where did they go?" he stuttered.

I was so scared I couldn't answer.

Peter's hair was practically standing on end. "Let's get out of here," he said, and the two of us clattered back down the rickety stairs, letting the hatch slam shut behind us.

Books by M. M. Ragz

Eyeballs for Breakfast
Sewer Soup
Stiff Competition

Available from MINSTREL Books

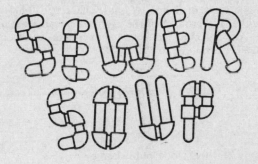

M. M. RAGZ

A
MINSTREL®
BOOK

PUBLISHED BY POCKET BOOKS

New York   London   Toronto   Sydney   Tokyo   Singapore

A MINSTREL PAPERBACK *ORIGINAL*

 A Minstrel Book published by
POCKET BOOKS, a division of Simon & Schuster Inc.
1230 Avenue of the Americas, New York, NY 10020

ISBN: 0-671-75881-0

First Minstrel Books printing March 1992

10 9 8 7 6 5 4 3 2

A MINSTREL BOOK and colophon are registered trademarks
of Simon & Schuster Inc.

Printed in the U.S.A.

With love to good friends

Stephanie Dahl
Kit Howard
Barbara Schwartz

for all your help and encouragement

Special thanks to

James C. Killian, Chief, Division of Environmental Planning
Cape Cod National Seashore

for sharing your time and technical knowledge

Cast of Characters

Murphy: He spends February vacation trying to figure out what's floating around in the fog—and in the soup

Peter: A horror-movie fan. But can he handle it when life starts to look like the movies?

Ashley: Murphy's number-one rival. Will her curiosity get her into more than she bargained for?

Abigail: Oldest of the three sisters, nicknamed "the Beacon." A terrific teller of tales, but how much is tale and how much is truth?

Bernice: The quiet twin who recently returned to live with her sisters. What secrets do those sad eyes hide?

Cecily: The dramatic twin who was once an actress. She still loves to perform, but how much is an act?

Albert Stark: An old sea captain. Do the X's on his mysterious maps lead to pirate treasure, graves, or something even more sinister?

James Killeran: An aggressive young ranger who wants to get the job done. Says nothing will stand in his way—not even ghosts. But what about the sisters?

Chapter

ONE

I was still miles from home. The wind picked up, rustling the dry marsh grass and kicking up the sand. What had started as a breeze was howling to a storm. The fog crawled along the path and swirled around my ankles like a gray ghost. I could hear the ocean thundering against the distant sand dunes.

"Suddenly darkness struck—not the black darkness of night, but an eerie gray caused by fog and storm. If I wasn't careful, I'd lose the path. I stopped to get my bearings, but in turning to look around, I lost my sense of direction.

"A light flashed through the gloom—and was gone. It flashed again—gone. Again—the old lighthouse on Deadman's Bluff. But it hadn't worked in years, not since the body of old Doc Porter had been found mangled in its tower.

"The ghostly fingers of the fog reached around my wrist, a twig snapped behind me, and I heard a low moan. As I started to run toward the light, a voice pierced the fog and said—"

1

"Murphy! I'm talking to you."

I caught my breath and whirled around, dropping the book I had been reading in my family room.

"Mom," I hollered. "Don't you know better than to go sneaking up on someone, scaring them half to death?"

"Sneaking up? *Sneaking?* Young man, I've been trying to get your attention for the last five minutes. What are you so wrapped up in?" She picked the book up off the floor and looked at it. *"The Ghost of Deadman's Bluff.* Sounds scary."

"It is. I'm reading it for a book report. It's due after winter vacation."

She smiled. "Speaking of winter vacation, I have a wonderful surprise for you. We're not staying home—we're going to take a real vacation this year."

"You're kidding!" I could hardly believe what I was hearing. We always spent February vacation in Westford—cold, damp, dark Westford, Connecticut. And now Mom was talking vacation.

"Don't tell me," I said, closing my eyes and letting my mind drift. "Let me guess. Florida? California? A cruise? No—I know. You and Dad were looking through those Club Med brochures. The ones with the separate clubs for kids. That's it! Right, Mom? Right?"

"Well, not quite. Actually, your father isn't coming with us. I'm going to Cape Cod and you're coming with me."

Her words hit me like a cold wind. "We're going *where?* Mom, it's the middle of February. People don't go to Massachusetts in February. They go south. And what do you mean 'Dad's not coming'?"

"I've been invited to attend a conference—all expenses paid. So Mrs. Douglas and I thought that you and her daughter Ashley—"

"*Ashley?* Mrs. Douglas? What are you talking about?"

"Mrs. Douglas and I are going to the same conference. We talked it over and decided to treat you and Ashley to a vacation."

I pinched myself. I knew I was in the middle of some horrible nightmare. It must have been the sausage on the pizza I had last night.

Ashley and I were class-A rivals. She thought of herself as being princess of the gifted and acted as if I were her toad. I had a better brain than she did, a better sense of humor, more friends, and a whole lot more personality. The only one who didn't seem to realize that was Ashley herself.

"Mom, you know I'd do almost anything for you. I'll clean my room. I'll shop for clothes. But please don't ask me to go anywhere with Ashley Douglas."

"I'm sorry you feel that way. But it's already been decided. We have the reservations. We leave this Sunday. I was hoping you'd be excited about it—I'm sure Ashley is—but if you're not, that's okay, too. We're going. It'll be fun. You'll see."

I had to think fast. "I'll stay home with Dad. You go ahead and have a nice time."

"Sorry, Murphy. Dad and I talked it over, and we think it would be best for you to come with me."

I could run away from home, or I could join the navy, or I could get kidnapped. I could . . . "Could Peter come? Could I ask my best friend to come with me? Please? Don't make me spend a whole week alone with Ashley Douglas."

3

Mom started to look all serious. "Well, I suppose so. One more child shouldn't be a problem, and if it would make you happy—"

"You're terrific, Mom. I'm going to call Peter right now." Maybe it wouldn't be so bad. We had spent a week last summer on Cape Cod, in Hyannis, which is a pretty big city.

As I picked up the phone I asked, "Are we staying at the same hotel in Hyannis as we did before? Peter's going to love the game room and the indoor pool." I started to dial.

Mom came over and hung up the phone. "Before you call Peter, I think there are a few things I should tell you. The conference is not in Hyannis. It's farther north in a small town called Eastham at the Sheraton, but we're not staying there."

She paused for a minute and then continued. "Mrs. Douglas's cousin has some friends who own an old captain's house—it's an inn, actually. During the summer they rent out rooms. They're closed to tourists now, but Mrs. Douglas called them and they agreed to let us stay with them. They're three elderly sisters. Mrs. Douglas and I will be busy most of the day. The women will provide some supervision for you and Ashley—and Peter, if he comes along."

I put on my I-don't-believe-what-I'm-hearing face. "Are you trying to say there won't even be a game room? Or a pool? Or a mall?"

She took a deep breath. "Not even a TV, Murphy. But the inn is on the National Seashore, so there will be lots of nature and walking trails and history, and maybe, if the weather's good, bikes to ride. It'll be a

4

week of fresh air and exercise—a wonderful experience. And very educational."

"Oh, *terrific!* What can I possibly tell Peter that would make him want to come?"

She thought a few seconds, then bent over and picked up my book. "The inn is near the ocean. It's an old captain's house. I'm sure it's not very spooky or mysterious, but there is a lighthouse nearby and I'm sure the three of you could find things to do. You'll find a way to make it sound exciting to Peter."

She was right, of course. I had a terrific imagination. I waited until she left the room, picked up the phone, and dialed Peter's number. When he answered I said, "Peter, wait until you hear where I'm going next week." And I talked vaguely about lighthouses and ghosts and disappearances.

He started to ask me a million questions about the trip so I said, "Listen, Peter. I've got a great idea. I'm not sure Mom will go for it, but if you'd like, maybe I could talk her into letting you come along." I held my breath.

I didn't have to wait long. In a matter of minutes he was practically begging me to let him come, so I said, "Let me talk to Mom. Like I said, I'm not sure she'll go for it, but I can be pretty persuasive. I'll call you back later."

Chapter

TWO

As we packed our suitcases into Mrs. Douglas's station wagon on Sunday morning, Peter pulled me aside. "You didn't tell me Ashley was coming."

"I didn't?"

"No, you didn't. What's the big idea?"

"No big idea. I thought I told you. Her mom and my mom are going to the same conference. We'll be pretty much alone all day. Maybe we can ditch her and go exploring."

He got a gleam in his eye and a smile on his face. He was about to say something when Ashley sashayed over to us.

"Isn't this neat? We get to spend the whole vacation by ourselves. It'll be so educational. Maybe we could even write a report and get some extra credit for school. My mother got me all kinds of information on the history of the Cape and the National Seashore and Eastham."

I almost choked. Peter looked like he was about to

change his mind and stay home. "She's kidding, Peter. You know girls and their warped sense of humor."

She gave me a dirty look. "Who are you calling warped? You're just jealous because I'm smarter than you, and you don't want me to show you up in front of Peter. This is an educational trip. I just thought we could work together on some kind of project. Peter can help. Even though he's technically not in the gifted group like we are, he's pretty smart, aren't you, Peter?"

That Ashley. She had about as much tact as a steamroller.

"Come on, Peter," I said quickly, pulling him away from Ashley. "Don't pay any attention to her. We'll figure out a way to lose her," I whispered.

The three of us piled into the back of Mrs. Douglas's station wagon, and, as we got on the highway, Ashley started to read out loud about Cape Cod.

Peter was plugged into his Walkman, and I was reading.

Ashley opened one of her books. "Listen to this about all the shipwrecks," she practically shouted. When we didn't pay attention, she pulled Peter's earphones off his head and grabbed my book.

We struggled with her for a minute until Mom turned around and said sharply, "That's enough."

"Ashley started it," I said. "Tell her to read to herself."

Mom reached back and took my book and Peter's Walkman. "It's a long ride. Why don't you listen for a few minutes?"

Peter and I put on the most bored faces we could manage as Ashley flipped through the book and read,

"Pirate gold. According to legend, Captain Kidd's treasure was buried on Cape Cod and still hasn't been recovered. Once a year only, it is whispered, do you stand a chance of finding Captain Kidd's treasure—" She stopped abruptly and said, "Yuck, I'm not reading this."

Before she had a chance to turn the page, Peter grabbed the book and kept reading. ". . . on the seventh night of the seventh moon. And the moon must be full. At the stroke of midnight you slay a sheep and let the blood flow from the cut to the spot where the gold is buried, and you start digging—"

Ashley put her hands over her ears. "That's the most disgusting thing I've ever heard."

"But maybe it's true," I said. "Maybe we could come back on July 7th, kill a sheep, drain its blood, and get rich."

"That's the grossest idea you've ever had," said Ashley, looking like she wanted to puke. "Besides, it's just superstition."

Peter winked at me. "You were the one who said it was educational, Ashley."

"Well, you can't believe *everything* you read, you know," she said, grabbing back the book and putting it on the bottom of her pile. "Let's read about something else."

"Let's play license plate poker instead," I suggested.

"Sounds like fun," Peter said.

"Sounds childish," said Ashley. "I'd rather read."

Chapter

THREE

I must have dozed for a while. When I woke up, I heard Mom ask, "Are you sure we're on the right road?"

Mrs. Douglas had slowed down to thirty-five and was straining over the steering wheel to see the road ahead of her.

"I've never seen fog roll in so fast," said Mrs. Douglas. "Here it is, only two o'clock in the afternoon, and it's worse than driving at night. I can't see more than a few feet in front of us. It's like driving through soup."

"I see a sign ahead," I yelled.

Mrs. Douglas slowed down even more and Ashley read, NATIONAL SEASHORE VISITOR'S CENTER.

"That's where we turn," said Mom. "Then we take a quick left, go to the end and take another right."

We plodded along through the fog, but after a few more minutes, Mrs. Douglas stopped, threw her hands up and said, "I give up. I don't know where we are."

9

All of a sudden a bright white light swept through the fog and was gone. Then a red light swept by. "Isn't the inn near the ocean?" Mom asked. The white light flashed again.

"A lighthouse," I said. "This must be the right road. Just go a little farther, Mrs. Douglas."

She inched along slowly.

"There it is," Mom said. "I see a sign that says, THE INN OF THE THREE SISTERS. Turn here."

We went slowly up a twisting, sandy driveway that seemed to go on for miles. Tall pine trees stood on both sides.

"Creepy," I said.

"Interesting," said Ashley.

"I know you'll have a wonderful time," said Mrs. Douglas. "I'm sure the three sisters are looking forward to spending time with you. They must be lonely out here by themselves."

"Are they actually sisters?" asked Ashley. "The Inn of the Three Sisters is really run by three sisters?"

"That's right," said Mrs. Douglas. "My cousin Geraldine said they've lived very interesting lives. Two were married, but their husbands both died. One of them had a career in the theater—an actress. They're all in their seventies now. They came back to the Cape to live in this captain's house that's been in the family for generations. Maybe you could get them to tell you the stories of their lives."

Peter leaned close to me. "You're going to owe me a lot of favors," he whispered in my ear. "I can't believe you talked me into this."

"You're my best friend," I whispered back. "You

would have come even if you knew Ashley was coming, wouldn't you?"

"I guess so," he grumped. "But you still owe me."

We pulled around another bend in the driveway and the house suddenly appeared before us, rising out of the fog.

"Wow, neat," said Peter. "Look at that place. It looks like something out of a horror movie."

He was right. It was a gigantic old gray house with a wide porch wrapped around it, towers with pointed roofs, and tall narrow windows. The shades were all down and some of the shutters were closed, giving it the look of a sleeping giant. On top of the roof was a railing. As we got out of the car I asked Peter, "What's that thing up there on the roof? A deck?"

Ashley started to laugh. "Don't you know a widow's walk when you see one?"

I gave a disgusted look. "No. Because I've never seen one. And how do you know what it is?"

"It's in the book I was reading. They were built for the wives of sea captains. When the captain was supposed to come home after months or years at sea, his wife would go up to the roof and try to spot his ship. Sometimes they would walk up there for hours."

"I'll bet when there's no fog you can see for miles from up there," said Peter.

"I haven't finished explaining, Peter," said Ashley. "Don't interrupt."

"Well, par-don me!" said Peter.

"Anyway, there's a legend in this book about a woman named Violet Hapgood who actually saw her husband's ship being wrecked in a storm off the coast.

11

She went crazy and jumped off the roof to her death. For years after that, neighbors would swear they saw Violet on foggy, stormy nights, pacing her widow's walk, looking for her husband.''

Peter was staring at the house, grinning. "Boy, oh boy, maybe this old place really is haunted," he said.

Chapter

FOUR

Mom must have pushed the doorbell a solid minute before the front door opened—just a crack.

"What do you want?" asked a loud, scratchy voice.

"I'm Geraldine's cousin," Mrs. Douglas said. "I called about renting some rooms for my friend and me. And for our children?"

I was getting cold standing on the porch, and I pulled up the hood of my parka. The door opened a little wider. A woman who was only about my height glared at us through thick glasses. She looked old enough and mean enough to be a close relative of the Wicked Witch of the West. A thin, sad-faced lady was standing behind her.

"No one called. And we don't accept children or pets—ever!" She started to close the door.

"But I called last week," Mrs. Douglas said hurriedly. "Whoever I spoke with said it would be fine."

Suddenly, another woman with curly red hair opened the door wide and said, "For heaven's sake, Abigail.

You'll be asking for a passport next. Can't you see they're freezing out there? And you're letting all the heat out. Come in. Come in.'' She shook hands quickly with each of us. ''My name is Cecily.''

We stepped past Abigail, who looked like she wanted to turn us into toads, and followed Cecily, who bounced along and whistled. ''You must be pooped after that long drive,'' she said.

We walked into a room that looked like something out of our history book. Heavy drapes blocked the sunlight. Overstuffed couches and chairs crowded the wooden floor that was covered with braided rugs. Old-fashioned lamps with colored glass shades glowed on tables. Everything smelled like dust, and Peter sneezed three times.

''Please, sit down,'' said Cecily, and we sank into deep cushioned sofas that raised a little more dust.

''I hope you were expecting us,'' said Mrs. Douglas. ''Geraldine said you might enjoy having us stay with you—''

''Of course we were expecting you,'' interrupted Cecily. ''Don't pay any attention to Abigail. She's always grouchy in the winter.'' She winked at us and said in a loud whisper, ''It's her arthritis acting up, you see, and she's always cranky when her bones ache.''

Abigail snorted and squinted at us, the frown lines getting deeper. She wore a dark brown sweater and skirt, thick stockings, and heavy shoes that clomped when she walked.

The other sister, who hadn't yet said anything, was all dressed in gray and had a wool shawl pulled around her shoulders. She kept fiddling with the fringe on the

14

cape and reminded me of a nervous bird ready to fly away at the slightest noise.

"Mercy me," Cecily said. "It sure feels gloomy in here." And she bustled around raising shades and pushing back the drapes. She was a lot friendlier than the other two. By her bright clothes and her long, fluttery eyelashes, I knew she was the one who had been an actress.

"We appreciate your letting us stay with you," Mom said. "I'm Kate Darinzo, this is my son Murphy and his friend Peter. And this is Nora's daughter, Ashley." She stood up while she introduced us.

Cecily bowed slightly. "Welcome, Mrs. Darinzo."

"Please call me Kate." Mom looked around. "I'm sorry, I didn't get all of your names."

"Just call me Cecily," she said. "And that's my oldest sister Abigail, the one who tried to freeze you out. And that's my older sister Bernice," she said, pointing to the birdlike woman who pulled her shawl closer around her. "She's a little older than I am—exactly one hour older, isn't that right, Bernice? We're twins, you see, but I was last one born so I'm the baby sister."

I looked closely from one face to the other. Sure enough, they were twins—same face, same height and weight. But that's where the resemblance stopped.

"It's real easy to remember which of us is which," Cecily continued. "Abigail begins with the letter A, and she's the oldest. She's always been our guide, our beacon. Then there's B for Bernice and C for Cecily— that's me. We had a younger brother after that and his name was David, but he died when he was little and it made my mother sad so she stopped having babies. She likely would have gone all the way to Z if she—"

"Oh, for goodness' sake, Cecily," barked Abigail. "Don't you ever get tired of talking?" She shook her head. "Since it looks like these folks are determined to stay, show them to their rooms so they can get ready for supper. Supper is always at five-thirty sharp. If you're not there, we eat without you. You're on your own for breakfast and lunch."

"Kate and I are attending the conference at the Sheraton," said Mrs. Douglas. "We won't be here for meals, as I explained over the phone. I'm not sure who I talked to, but whoever it was said that the children could have all their meals here. We'll gladly pay extra. I was told that you'd be happy to keep an eye on them, since Kate and I will be gone most of the day."

By the way the three sisters looked at each other, I knew right away that Mrs. Douglas had talked to Cecily. Of the three, she was the only one who acted like she wanted company.

"How long are you staying?" asked Abigail.

"Just a few days," said Mom. "We're planning to leave on Thursday morning."

"As long as the young ones behave. We're getting too old to be baby-sitters." She glared at Cecily. "We're closed for the season and we only rent rooms in the summer. But if we said we will, then we will."

It looked to me like they were more in need of babysitting than we were, but I wasn't about to open my mouth. I wasn't going to risk getting turned into a toad.

We got our bags out of the station wagon and followed Cecily—up three flights of winding stairs, down a whole maze of hallways, around corners, and finally to our rooms.

"How are we ever going to find our way around?" I whispered to Peter.

"I don't know," Peter whispered back. "But at least it shouldn't be too hard to lose Ashley."

"I heard that, Peter," Ashley said, coming up right behind us. "And you won't have to worry about getting lost. I have a wonderful sense of direction. Stick with me."

Peter just rolled his eyes.

"We'll put the boys in here," Cecily said, pushing open a heavy wooden door. "It's a room overlooking the ocean. Better air it out. It hasn't been used since last summer and it's a little stuffy."

And creepy. A small shaft of sunlight peeked through the cracks of the drawn curtains. Dust floated in the light and I imagined spiders and bugs that had worked through the winter. Cecily pulled back the drapes and opened a window. "Oh—the fog has lifted. Just look at this view. You can see the ocean from here. And hear it. Listen—shhh."

We all crowded around the window. The surf rolled along a strip of beach. Mrs. Douglas stretched her arms out wide and gasped, "It's beautiful—the magic of the Cape. Nature at its most wonderful."

Peter and I made lemon-eating faces.

Cecily opened another door. "Ashley can have this room next to the boys, and the mothers can share the room across the hall."

I went into our room and opened a small door that I thought was a closet, but it was a tiny area with iron steps going up. "What's this?"

Cecily came over. "That leads to the widow's walk. But don't go up there. The steps are narrow and the

17

railing needs fixing. That's one of the reasons Abigail has her no-children-allowed rule. The house is old and delicate in spots.''

Peter winked at me and whispered, "And we wouldn't want to disturb Violet on her night walks, right, Murphy?"

Thinking about a ghost walking over our heads made me shudder.

Cecily looked at a huge wristwatch she was wearing and said, "Now hurry and get settled. It's almost time for dinner and the Beacon will take a fit if you're late."

"Who?" asked Ashley, looking confused.

"The Beacon—Abigail—our guiding light. She's bossy and she's cranky sometimes, but I don't know what Twin and I would do without her." And with that, she bobbed out of the room.

"Weird," said Peter.

"I think she's nice," said Ashley.

"You would," I said. "The Alphabet Sisters. They're all a little nuts if you ask me."

"What do you mean Alphabet Sisters?" asked Peter.

"You know—'A' is for Abigail, 'B' is for Bernice and 'C' is for Cecily—oldest to youngest."

Peter spun his finger in a circle. "Like I said—*weird*. Come on, let's go eat. I'm hungry."

Suddenly I heard a thumping over our heads, like someone was up on the roof. I looked at Peter. "What's that? The wind?"

"I don't know, but I'm not hanging around to find out. Let's go." And we walked a little faster.

Chapter

FIVE

Mom and Mrs. Douglas didn't stay with us for dinner. They were off to the hotel to register for the conference and said they'd eat there. "Behave," they both said as they left the three of us sitting at one end of a long dining room table.

Abigail set small bowls of a steamy, dark, thick substance in front of us. Peter, Ashley, and I stirred through the guck with our spoons. Strange black things emerged from the bottom, hung on top of the sludge, and sank again to the bottom. Abigail walked to the other end of the table to serve the three of them.

"Oh, YUCK!" I whispered.

"What do you suppose it is?" Peter asked.

"It looks like sewer slime."

"I can't eat this," Ashley whined.

Abigail, having served everyone, stood at the head of the table. "Let's all bow our heads and say a silent thank you for the food we are about to eat."

Peter started to put his head down, but popped it

straight up again. He leaned toward me and whispered, "It smells funny. Kind of like my locker did after I forgot my dirty gym clothes in it over Christmas vacation."

I bowed my head and sniffed. It was definitely different.

Abigail, satisfied, I guess, that everyone was thankful enough, cleared her throat and said in a loud voice, "I expect you children to make clean plates. This is yankee bean soup, our own recipe. We've added fish for protein. It's a stick-to-the-ribs and make-you-grow kind of soup."

I had to think of something. I'm not a fussy eater, but I wasn't going to eat sewer soup.

"Excuse me," I said. "I can't eat the soup. I'm . . . ah . . . I'm allergic to beans."

"Yeah, me, too," added Peter. Then he added under his breath, "They make me pass the gas." And we all giggled.

Abigail got up, walked to our end of the table, and stood between Peter and me. She put a hand on our shoulders. With just the slightest squeeze she said, "Children must learn to cultivate new tastes. The problem with our society is that we're letting our children go soft—too much peanut butter and white bread. I used to tell my students when I was teaching that junk food leads to the jitters. And I will have no jittery children staying with us. Now eat your soup."

She was tough. And I suddenly realized I'd eat cooked rat if Abigail told us to.

We ate.

After dinner Abigail set down some rules for us for the week.

"Our food's not fancy, but it's healthy—good hot cereal for breakfast and there's always a pot of soup simmering on the stove—it'll make a good lunch." I felt sick.

"You will clean up after yourselves," she continued. "We tolerate no messes, especially from young people."

I felt like I was sitting at a desk and should fold my hands.

"You be sure to be in the house before it gets dark—that's around five—because when it gets dark around here, you can't see two inches in front of you. And watch for the fog. It's been rolling in early lately, and that can be worse than the dark for getting lost in. Is that clear?" she asked.

"Yes, ma'am," Ashley said. I was surprised to hear Ashley sound so meek.

"Excuse me," I said, and almost raised my hand.

"Yes, young man?"

"Are there some bikes we could use? Mrs. Douglas said something about bike trails, and maybe we could go exploring."

"It's the middle of winter. I don't think . . ."

Suddenly Cecily interrupted. "Oh, Abigail. For heaven's sake. Don't be such a stuffed shirt. This is not your classroom."

Abigail looked like she wanted to spit. Her mouth got all tight, and she screwed up her face and glared at Cecily.

Cecily just laughed. "Abby, I swear, your face is going to freeze like that some day. Poppa nicknamed you the Beacon because you were the oldest, but you don't have to be so bossy."

21

Abigail unscrewed her face a little and said, "I suppose there are some bikes. You'll have to get them from Captain Stark. He lives next door. He's got them fixed and oiled and locked up for the winter. They're for the summer guests, but you can use them—if you promise to be careful."

"We'll be careful," Peter and Ashley said together.

"Fine," said Abigail. "Stay close to the house, away from any main roads. And don't go anywhere there's a NO TRESPASSING sign. Lots of the houses and cottages around here are owned by summer people, and they don't want anyone snooping. Or doing damage. Is that clear?"

"Yes, Ma'am," the three of us answered.

"I will say it once more. If you see a NO TRESPASSING sign, you go the other way. I want no problems. Now—up to bed with you. Wash up, say your prayers, and go to bed."

"But it's not even seven o'clock," Peter protested.

"And it's vacation," Ashley added.

"I'll tell you what, kids," Cecily said. "Help me with the dishes, and after we finish up, we'll talk Abigail into telling us one of her stories." She came to our end of the table and started to clear the plates. When we didn't move to help, she bent down and whispered, "Maybe we can roast some marshmallows in the fireplace."

I looked at Peter. "What do you think?"

He stood up and started to stack plates. "It sure beats going to sleep at seven. I'll just pig out on marshmallows. Maybe I'll stuff some in my ears so I won't have to listen to boring old Abigail's boring old story."

Chapter

SIX

The fire crackled brightly in the huge stone fireplace. Abigail, seated in a chair by the fire, waited until Cecily turned down the only lamp in the room. Peter, Ashley, and I, stuffed with marshmallows, sat on the couch, ready to be bored to sleep. Bernice, shawl wrapped tightly around her, sat quietly in a chair across from Abigail. Cecily plunked herself down next to me on the couch, making us all squeeze together.

Abigail waited until the only sounds came from the fire, and then she leaned forward and said, "A long, long time ago—long before the government and the tourists wanted to destroy the natural beauty of the Cape— here—on this very spot—lived pirates."

"Pirates?" Ashley gasped.

"Oh, boy," said Peter.

Cecily giggled and said, "Oh, goody—the pirates."

Abigail raised her voice just enough to quiet us down. "Not pirates, exactly. They were mooncussers, which—" and she paused, put up an index finger to stop all our questions, and continued, "which I shall explain as the story goes on. Now hush while I tell it."

We hushed. The firelight threw long shadows around the room, dark shadows that flickered and danced.

Abigail settled back in the chair, closed her eyes, and began talking quietly. "Loneliness can do strange things to people. And there was nothing lonelier than a Cape Cod winter a few hundred years ago. The men who lived near the sea were sailors and spent months at a time away from their families.

"Legend tells of a young girl named Sara Ann Snow who lived with her mother and father and older brother Erik. Her father and Erik were both seamen, and every fall, as the leaves began to turn to gold, she kissed them both good-bye and watched them sail off to sea. They were bound for distant shores and never returned until the leaves began to green again in the spring.

"One fall, when Sara Ann was just about your age"— Abigail pointed a crooked finger at Ashley—"a fear grew in her heart. She threw her arms around her brother and cried, 'Don't go. I am afraid I will never see you again.'

" 'We always return,' said her brother, hugging her. 'We always come home safely.'

"Sara Ann clung to him. Then she took off a gold locket from around her neck and said, 'Keep this with you always. It will bring you back to me.'

"Erik put the locket into his uniform pocket and said, 'Now you know I will have to return. This locket belonged to our great-great-grandmother and has been passed down from generation to generation. Legend says that it can never be lost and will always return to its owner.' And he left.

"Winter passed into spring and spring passed into summer. Every day Sara Ann waited for her father's ship to return. But summer passed again into fall and fall into winter, and the ship never came.

"Her mother wept. 'Your father and your brother are lost at sea and will never return to us.'

"Sara Ann refused to give up hope. 'Erik will return,' was all she said.

"Many years passed. Hard winters and dry summers caused the small seaside village to become poorer and poorer. Sara Ann and her mother, along with their neighbors, became beach scavengers. They gathered wood for fire and shellfish for food.

"Because there were no lighthouses to help passing ships, many were wrecked on the treacherous shoals. The shipwrecks were a terrible thing, but the people came to depend on them for their survival. Cargo would wash ashore—barrels of coffee and tobacco, fruit and spices, wood and cloth.

"Some of the women picked over the bodies of the dead sailors for jewels or clothing, but Sara Ann could not pick the pockets of dead men.

"On a dark February day, a small spidery man moved into a shack near Sara Ann and her mother. He owned an old white horse with two red eyes. He called himself Reverend Stone, but people whispered that he was a man of the devil, and his horse had eaten so much cemetery grass that she knew ghosts and spirits.

"Reverend Stone combed the beach with the rest of them, but he was impatient waiting for ships to wreck. One day, after months of calm without a wreck, he said,

'You are fools, and you will die. Think of yourselves and your children. I will show you a way to riches.' He locked himself in his shack, and those who dared go near said they heard strange chants and evil words.

"The wind blew full gale that night. Black fields of clouds hung over the sky. No rain fell. Hurricane waves beat up the beach and churned the ocean into a white madness. The people gathered on the beach around the figure of the small, dark man and watched as he tied two lanterns on his horse—one on the tail and one on the mane. He gave lanterns to the others and said, 'Follow me,' and whipped his horse, driving her cruelly over the hissing sand.

"Soon a ship, caught in the storm and thinking the lights to be those of another ship, followed the false signals and wrecked on the shoals. All the sailors drowned, but the cargo of gold and jewels made the people rich.

"Night after dark night, under the spell of greed and evil, they followed Reverend Stone and his evil white horse. Many ships wrecked while the horse neighed joyously and her wicked master and the people rejoiced.

"But sometimes, when they stood with their devil lights on the dark shore, the moon would break out from behind a cloud. Then the captain of the ship would see the land and steer his craft safely away. The people would stomp their feet and shake their fists and curse at the moon. And so they were called mooncussers, for moonlit nights held no profit.

"Sara Ann did not like what greed was doing to her neighbors, and she refused to carry a lantern. But the others were angry with her and said to her mother, 'If Sara Ann does not help, we will give you no food. You will live as outcasts, poor and alone. Sara Ann must help.'

"Her mother begged and pleaded and finally Sara Ann agreed. On the night of February 25th she took up a lantern and joined the others. She watched as a ship, a dark spot on the sea, turned toward the lights. She watched as the ship rolled on its side, high seas pounding over its deck, great masts and sails torn apart. And she watched as barrels and crates and poor dead sailors began to wash up on the shore.

" 'Pick the pockets of the dead, Sara Ann,' hissed the skinny little Reverend in her ear, 'or else you shall have nothing.' "

Suddenly Abigail paused in her story, closed her eyes, and rested her head on the back of her chair. Shadows flickered all around us and a clock ticked somewhere in the distance. We sat spellbound. Even Cecily looked wide-eyed, and I wondered why, since she'd probably heard the story before. Bernice's face was hidden in the shadows, so I couldn't tell what she was feeling.

The silence dragged on. I was getting goosebumps, but I didn't move. Finally Abigail opened her eyes and continued.

"Slowly Sara Ann walked down the beach, avoiding the bodies that lay on their backs with their eyes staring. She finally came to the body of a man face down in the sand, kneeled by him, and put her hand into his pocket. She pulled out five gold coins, a pocket watch, and a folded paper which she thrust into her own pocket. She reached into his other pocket and her hand closed around a small round object attached to a chain. Trembling, she pulled out her hand and opened her fist. By the dim light of her lantern she saw a gold locket,

27

the same gold locket she had given her brother so many years ago.

"She fumbled in her pocket for the paper, brought her lantern close and read, 'Dear Sara Ann. We were lost at sea and found. When I come home we will celebrate the magic of the locket. I know it is the locket that brings us together.'

"She turned the body over and looked into the face of her dead brother, dead because of her, dead because of her evil light.

"She did not weep. She put the locket around her neck and walked toward the thundering waves, murmuring, 'Together, we will be together.'

"It did not take long for the others to realize the horror of this wreck, for many of their own men lay dead upon the beach, and the women, weeping and wailing, rushed toward the sea, trying to save Sara Ann.

"Reverend Stone mounted his horse and called against the roaring wind, a shriek devoured by the sea. At that moment the moon came dazzling through the clouds. Lunar madness seized the horse. Wildly neighing, she swam toward the center of the moonfall, and horse and rider were washed away."

Abigail stopped talking. The room was dead quiet. Only the fire, burned down to its end, sputtered and crackled. Then, from the corner of the room where Bernice had sat like a stone the whole time, came the faint whisper of a voice. "And on dark nights in February, when the beach is covered by storm or fog, the haunted spirits of the mooncussers must once again walk the beach, carrying lanterns and torches, looking for their men. But they walk alone, forever, never to find them. Doomed forever to walk the beach one month a year, the women swing their cursed lanterns and hope beyond hope that the moon will come out and save the ship."

I felt prickles all up and down my back. I didn't dare move.

It was Cecily who finally broke the spell. She giggled and said, "But it never does, you know. The moon, I mean. It can never save that ship. Or those women."

Abigail stood up and snapped on the light. I squinted in the glare. "Now that's just plain nonsense. All this talk about hauntings and ghosts. Bernice, you'll be giving the young ones nightmares."

She turned to us. "Don't you believe a word of it. About the ghosts, that is. Some say that the legend of the mooncussers is true. But the ghosts and the lights on the beach? Just talk!"

It got quiet again. Then suddenly, without warning, from somewhere out in the night, came a scream—a long, wailing screech. My heart stopped. Ashley gasped. Peter looked pale. "What was that?" we all asked at once.

"What was what?" asked Cecily.

"That scream," I said, not believing she didn't hear it.

"That bloodcurdling howl," added Ashley.

Abigail was plumping up the cushions on the chair. "Oh, that's just raccoons fighting. Or a screech owl. You city kids have to get used to strange noises around. Can't let your imaginations run away with you."

Just then Mom and Mrs. Douglas walked in.

"Hi, kids," Mom said. "Having a good time? What's the matter? You look as if you've seen a ghost."

Peter started to laugh and said, "We're just getting a history lesson about Cape Cod."

Chapter

SEVEN

I had a restless night. I kept waking up, thinking I was hearing something—something like Violet walking over my head or old Reverend Stone's horse neighing.

The third time I woke up it was from a rumbling noise, like a freight train in the distance. I got out of bed and walked over to the window. The night was black, so black that it looked solid. I strained hard to see something—anything, and was about to give up and go back to bed when I saw specks of light moving in the distance. I rubbed my eyes and looked again. They were still there—lights on the beach, swaying slowly, like people carrying lanterns.

Then the moon peeked out from behind a cloud, throwing a ghostly glow over everything. And there— down on the beach—sure enough—four shadowy figures carried lights. It had to be a dream, but it didn't feel like a dream. Mooncussers? It couldn't be. That was just Abigail's story. Yet someone or something was out there, and she said they walked the beach in February.

I ran over to where Peter was sleeping.

"Peter, wake up," I whispered loudly. But he just rolled over and groaned.

I leaned over him and said right into his ear, "Peter, there are ghosts on the beach." I turned the light on next to his bed.

He sat up, rubbing his eyes. "Murphy? Are you crazy? It's the middle of the night. What did you wake me up for?"

"Ghosts. On the beach."

"What are you talking about? What ghosts?"

I pointed to the window. "Out there. On the beach. The mooncussers are walking. Hurry up."

"Murphy, you're crazy. Go back to bed." And he turned off the light and rolled over.

I put the light on again and pulled the covers off the bed. "I'm not crazy. Look for yourself."

He slowly pulled himself up, plopped his feet on the floor, and followed me to the window. But with the light still on in the room, and the night outside so black, we couldn't see anything, so I ran back and turned off the light. "See them?" I asked, hurrying back to the window.

He just turned and looked at me.

"I told you. Down there." And I peered out the window and came face to face with nothing but the solid black night pressed against the window.

"They're gone," I said, disappointed.

"Yeah, right. They're gone. If you ask me, you had an overdose of Abigail's ghost story. I'm going back to bed. And don't wake me up again. Got it, Murphy?"

He clomped across the room, fell into bed, and

wrapped himself in his blanket, asleep before I could say another word.

I looked out the window. I thought I could see another light in the distance, but I couldn't be sure. Peter was probably right—Abigail's story and her sewer soup were making me see things that weren't there. I climbed back into bed, tossed and turned awhile, and finally fell asleep.

When we went down for breakfast the next morning, Abigail was in the kitchen, standing over the old black stove, stirring a spoon in an iron pot. Bernice stood next to her.

"I'm so glad you're back," Abigail was saying to Bernice. "Maybe you can help. Lord knows Cecily's no help—she's too dramatic. And Albert's starting to talk crazy—wanting to rush things. And now these children—"

The three of us stood there, looking at each other. Ashley whispered, "Who's Albert?"

Peter just shrugged his shoulders.

"And what's he trying to rush?" Ashley whispered, a little too loudly this time, because Abigail turned around suddenly and saw us. Her glasses were all steamed and her wooden spoon dripped thick grayish-brown globs on the worn linoleum floor. I almost expected it to burn and bubble through.

As the fog cleared from her glasses, she scowled at us and asked, "How long have you three been standing there?" She looked mad enough to come over and bop us with her spoon.

"We just walked in," said Ashley cheerily. "We didn't hear a thing you said." Peter poked her in the ribs.

We stood there like three lumps while Abigail scowled at

us. "Sit down," she finally said. "I'll dish you each out a big bowl of oatmeal." Suddenly I didn't feel hungry. Oatmeal! Gray, globby oatmeal.

Just then Cecily came bustling in. "Hi, kids. How about some breakfast? It's a beautiful day out there."

"They're having oatmeal," Abigail grunted from the stove without turning around.

Cecily laughed. "Don't be silly, Abigail. It's too warm out for oatmeal. We're all having cereal—cold, sugary cereal—with lots of milk."

Abigail just shook her head.

Cecily dug out a box of Frosted Sugar Shocks from way back in the cupboard. It sure beat oatmeal, even though it was so sweet it made my teeth ache.

Bernice got herself a bowl of oatmeal and sat way down at the other end of the table.

"Could we go biking today?" Peter asked.

"Captain Stark has them locked up," said Abigail quickly. "And he's been feeling foul lately. I wouldn't go bothering him."

"Oh, Abigail. He's always foul," Cecily said.

Abigail just sighed. "Cecily, you'll drive me mad, I swear." She looked at us. "See Albert. He's got the bikes."

"Who, exactly, is Albert?" asked Ashley.

Abigail started to answer, but Cecily interrupted her, talking louder and faster. "Captain Albert Stark. He lives in the cottage next door. We all grew up together. In fact, Albert and Bernice were something of an item in high school, but then something happened, I'm not sure exactly what, and Bernice went away and finally married someone else and Albert just took to himself.

Bernice's husband died over a year ago, but Bernice just came back to live with us last month. Now maybe she and Albert can—"

Cecily's babbling was suddenly interrupted by a loud crash. Bernice, red-faced, was standing and trembling. A large pitcher of milk lay in pieces on the floor, and her chair was tipped over. She pulled her shawl tighter around her shoulders, looked at the mess, and quietly left the room.

Abigail glowered. "Sometimes you go too far."

Cecily, looking like a scolded schoolgirl, said, "I'm sorry, Abby. I am. You're right. I just get carried away. I'll go see Bernice." And she left.

Abigail started to clean up the spilled milk. "If you want to go biking, Albert's next door. He's a bit touchy, so don't cross him. Just mind your manners. There's a package in the hall you can take to him. The postman left it here by mistake. And remember—don't go near any NO TRESPASSING signs.

As we put on our coats in the front hall, Ashley asked, "What was all that about?"

"Who knows," Peter said. "If you ask me, these old girls have been alone too long. We'd better be on our guard. They might be dangerous."

"Don't be silly," Ashley said. "They may be a little strange, but they're harmless. I think they're kind of nice."

"Nice?" Peter laughed. "That Abigail has all the personality of an ax murderer. And how do we know what *really* happened to Bernice's husband? He could be buried in the basement. Don't let that little-old-lady act fool you. We could all wake up dead some morning."

"Oh, Peter," Ashley said, giggling. "There you go, sounding like those horror movies again. How can anyone wake up dead?"

"Exactly my point," said Peter, as he picked up the package shaped like a long cylinder that was addressed to Albert Stark and walked out the door.

Chapter

EIGHT

Captain Albert Stark's cottage looked more like a shack, and his yard looked like a junkyard—rusted cars up on blocks, boats with holes and peeling paint, scrap wood, broken tools. Long grass and scraggly weeds poked through everywhere.

Ashley and Peter were lagging behind, Ashley holding the long package, so that left me to knock on the door. No answer. I knocked again, a little harder this time.

"He's not here," Ashley said. "Let's go. This is a waste of time."

Peter disagreed. "We came for the bikes, and I don't want to leave without them. Let's peek in the window."

"What if he's there and just doesn't want company?" I asked.

"That's his problem. Come on." All of the shades were drawn, except for one in a front window that was halfway up. Peter pulled me over to the window, and we bent down and peered in. The window was dirty, but we could see that the inside was as cluttered as the outside—dirty dishes in the sink, newspapers piled high in corners, and a massive wooden table under the window covered with maps.

"And what do you two think you're doing?" boomed a voice behind us.

We wheeled around and came face to face with a man dressed in a navy blue short coat and a black captain's hat. He had skin like old leather, and eyes the color of a cloudy day. Long, wispy locks of gray hair and bushy eyebrows made him look like a picture out of an old book. In fact, he looked an awful lot like the picture I had in my mind of Reverend Stone.

The gray eyes turned dark, he raised his thick walking stick over his head as if he wanted to hit us, and snarled, "Somebody better do some fast talking if you want to be around for lunchtime." We were backed against the house with no way out. The stick threw a dense shadow across us.

Ashley, coming up behind him, carrying his package, said, "Excuse me, sir, are you Captain Albert Stark?"

He spun around and we rushed to Ashley's side in case she needed help.

She didn't.

"Would you really hit a girl?" Ashley asked. The two of them locked into a staring contest until he finally lowered his stick and said, "I am Captain Albert Stark. And I'm waiting for you to explain why you're snooping around my house." He spread his feet apart and put his hands on his hips.

Ashley imitated him. "We weren't snooping. We're guests at the Inn of the Three Sisters."

"Still doesn't give you a right to be peeping in windows." He turned to go into the house.

"Wait," yelled Ashley, running after him. "This package. It's for you. And we came to get some bikes."

He stopped, turned around, and saw the package Ashley was carrying. "Where'd you get that, girl?"

"The sisters. They asked us to bring it over. They said it got delivered there by mistake. Maybe it's a present. Is it your birthday or something? It's such a strange package. I wonder what's in it?"

He walked over and snatched the tube out of her hand. "You ask too many questions, girl. I don't like nosy people, and I especially don't like nosy children. Now state your business and be on your way."

"Cecily said we could borrow some bikes," I said quickly. I was anxious to get the bikes and get out of there. Albert Stark was not the most sociable person in the whole world.

"Figures," he grumbled. "Cecily's another one who won't mind her own business."

"She's very nice," said Ashley.

"I don't trust her. I don't trust any of them."

"I don't care what you say," Ashley said. "I like Cecily. She's the only one around here who seems to like company."

"We get enough company, as you call it, all summer. Tourists. Coming around with their squalling kids, littering up the beach. Then the government and their rangers, trying to change things." He paused for a minute and shook his head. Staring into space, he repeated, *"Always* trying to change things."

"What things?" asked Ashley.

His eyes snapped back to Ashley. "I told you, you ask too many questions. I'll get the bikes for you." He walked in his front door with the three of us right behind him. He went down a narrow hall and we waited in the front room.

We walked over to the table that was spread with maps. "Look at these," I said. "There must be fifty of them. Wonder what they are."

"Old maps," Peter said, bending over the table.

"Oh, that's brilliant," I said, laughing. "I can see that. But what are they maps of?"

Ashley spread one out that was partly rolled up. "It must be somewhere around here. This one has Eastham and the Atlantic Ocean on it."

"And this one has a bunch of X's on it, like a pirate's map," Peter said.

"And look at these three funny marks," I said, looking closely at another map. "Each one looks like part of a star."

Peter and Ashley looked over my shoulder. "That's strange," said Peter. "Those three funny star marks are on the map I was looking at, too."

"And on this one, too," Ashley said, walking over and unrolling her map again.

"Someone drew them in by hand," Peter said. "They're not really part of any of the maps."

Suddenly Albert Stark was standing over us like a tall shadow. "What are you doing in here?" he growled. "I thought I told you kids to wait outside."

For some reason, Albert didn't seem to scare Ashley. "No, you didn't. You didn't say anything. We just figured we were invited in."

"Well, you figured wrong. And what are you doing snooping around my things?"

"We weren't snooping. They're just maps. And who cares about your old maps anyway." Ashley tossed the one she was holding back on the table.

Albert glared at Ashley, but she just glared back at him. "Come on," he said, finally. "I'll get you the bikes." He locked the door behind him and took off at a brisk pace.

We followed him around the back of his house to a dilapidated shed. He unlocked a huge padlock, went inside for a minute, then stuck his head out of the door. "Well, what are you waiting for? You want bikes or not? I'll be danged if I do all the work getting them out."

"I wish you'd make up your mind, Captain Stark," Ashley said. "At the house we followed you in and you yelled at us. Now we wait politely outside, and you still have a fit."

Albert just snorted, but Peter whispered, "Knock it off, Ashley. We could be dealing with a maniac here. Get him mad enough and he'll lock us up and we'll never be found."

We went into the shed, and once our eyes got accustomed to the dim light, looked over the sad assortment of antique bikes.

"Hurry up," Albert said. "I don't have all day. There's ten good bikes here. Take your pick."

"Some pick," Ashley muttered.

Peter and I each wheeled out a blue bike. They had

fat tires, fat seats, and high chrome handlebars. Ashley came out with the same bike in red, but hers had a white straw basket and a bell.

As Albert locked up the shed, he said. "Keep the bikes at the inn until you go home. Stay away from NO TRESPASSING signs, and be careful. Just don't go poking around where you don't belong—it could be bad for your health."

"By the way," I said, as we were about to leave. "Do you own a horse, by any chance?"

He looked at me strangely. "Used to. Why do you ask?"

"No reason. You just remind me of someone I once heard of who lived around here and owned an old white horse."

"Wasn't me," he said. "Mine was black." He turned and walked away.

"What a weird guy," I said.

"You're not kidding," said Peter. "He may remind you of old Reverend Stone, but he reminds me of someone I saw in a movie once, an old guy who had a curse on him. At night he would turn into a beast and kill people. During the day he would find the bodies and bury them in his backyard. He had a map to show where all the graves were, and that's how he got caught."

"Between Albert and the Alphabet Sisters," I said, "I feel like we walked into a horror movie."

NINE

We rode down the long, sandy driveway. Peter and I raced each other and Ashley, behind us, kept jingling her stupid bell and yelling, "Wait for me, wait for me." We stopped at the end, trying to decide which way to go.

"The beach and the lighthouse are that way," I said. "Let's go take a look."

We pumped up a small hill that was much harder than it should have been because the bikes were heavy and had only one speed—slow. At the end of the street, the whole world opened up. There was nothing but sand, sky, and ocean, and a big red and white lighthouse up on the dunes with a road winding past it. About fifty feet in front of us the sand dropped off into a steep cliff. Below the cliff was the beach with the ocean surf roaring, the same sound I had heard in the middle of the night.

We stood at the edge of the cliff looking down. It felt like we were standing on the roof of a tall building.

"That's some drop," said Peter. He kicked a football-
sized rock off the edge and we watched as it created a
small avalanche of sand. A sign, half-buried, read ERO-
SION CONTROL—KEEP OFF.

"Let's take the bikes up to the lighthouse," I
suggested.

"Good idea," said Peter.

We pedaled up to the lighthouse, but it was surrounded with a high wire fence and a locked gate.
"Come on," said Peter. "Let's see where this road
goes."

We biked up past the lighthouse and came to a white
fence that blocked half the road. A sign on it said RESI-
DENTS ONLY.

"Well, that's it," said Ashley. "Let's go back."

"Why?" asked Peter.

"Because we're not residents," she said.

"Sure we are. For the week, anyway," I said. "You
can go back if you want to."

I thought it might be an easy way to get rid of Ashley,
but with Ashley, nothing is ever easy. We biked on and
she followed.

The road got narrower, and it was full of potholes
and tall brown weeds growing up through cracked asphalt. We passed some cottages that were boarded up—
summer homes of people who spent the winter in civili-
zation. The more we rode, the farther apart the cottages
were. Tall pine trees with scraggly dark green needles
threw bony limbs up toward the sky. Spiky brown grass
rustled in the wind and thick low bushes covered the
sandy ground on both sides.

The road was running parallel with the ocean and we
could see the sun sparkling off the water and hear the

rumbling surf. But we were high above it, with a steep cliff between us and the beach below. I hated to admit it, but Mrs. Douglas was right. This place was beautiful.

Then right ahead of us was another white fence with a big red sign that said DANGER. It blocked the whole road and we immediately saw why—on the other side of the fence most of the road had crumbled away down the steep cliff. Chunks of asphalt lay halfway down the sand embankment.

"Look at that," said Peter. "The whole road is just washed away here."

"Then we'll *have* to turn back," said Ashley. "And it's a good thing, too. We're too far away from anyone, and if we got into trouble, there would be no one around to help us."

"Don't be such a baby, Ashley," I said. "Lots of people must have come this way. There's a path right there, next to the broken road. Come on." I was suddenly feeling brave and daring, probably because Ashley wanted to go back.

But Peter hesitated. "That's not much of a path. Think we can get the bikes through?"

"Sure," I said, sounding more confident than I felt. I pushed my bike around the fence and, keeping my bike between me and the cliff, started to shove it along the sandy path. "It's only a little way. Look. The road starts again over there."

Peter was right behind me and I guess Ashley was behind him, but I had to concentrate on the narrow path so I didn't want to turn around to look.

It seemed to take hours. The bike kept getting bogged down in the sand or caught on the bushes. Brambles scratched my hands and once the rear wheel of the bike started to slide down the cliff. But when we were all safely on the other side, beyond a second white fence, I hollered, "We did it," and Peter and I slapped each other a high five.

Ashley mumbled, "Boys," but she was hanging in there with us, stubborn as ever. We looked back at the deep gorge we had passed and I was amazed at how steep it looked and how narrow the path was. "I just hope we make it back," said Ashley.

But Peter and I ignored her, hopped back on our bikes, and continued down the road. Suddenly, the paved road ended, turning into a sandy lane with deep ruts. It took a sharp turn to the left, away from the ocean. We were going deeper and deeper into unknown, uncivilized land, and I almost felt like we would meet up with Indians left over from hundreds of years ago.

The effort of riding the bikes on two loose sandy tire tracks was too much, so we got off and pushed. Even though it was February, I was getting hot and sweaty.

I was about to suggest we give up and go back when the road took another turn and we came to a run-down cabin built up on cement blocks. The shutters on the windows were closed, the gutters were half off, and the chimney was crumbling. A mouse ran from a downspout to an old pump and disappeared. I turned to Ashley, expecting her to scream, but she was just looking super disgusted.

The place gave me a creepy feeling—it was so old and isolated. I was about to say "Let's leave," when Ashley whispered, "There's a NO TRESPASSING sign. Let's get out of here."

That's all I needed. "No, let's get a closer look. The place looks deserted."

"Let's hide our bikes over there in the bushes," Peter suggested. "That way, if we see anyone, we can get away faster."

"Good idea," I said.

"Stupid idea," Ashley muttered, but she followed us anyway.

We hid the bikes and headed for the cabin. It looked ready to fall down any second, but we went up on the porch toward a window that had its shutter hanging half off.

Ashley stayed a few steps behind us. "Last time you two looked into a strange window, you almost got attacked. If anything happens this time, don't expect me to save you again."

Peter and I looked at each other and shrugged, then peeked through the window. What I saw sent a chill up my back. I jumped back and hurried off the porch.

"What? What is it?" asked Ashley. "What's in there?"

Peter, looking scared, came and stood next to me. He was breathing hard, like he had been running. "I don't know. It looks like a body."

Chapter

TEN

Ashley's mouth got all puckered and she clenched her hands by her side. "Peter Patterson. You're just trying to scare me. And it's not going to work!"

"He's not kidding, Ashley. Somebody's all crumpled up on the floor. An old woman. Dressed in real old-fashioned clothes. Let's get out of here."

Ashley kept frowning. "That's not funny, Murphy. And I'm not letting you two scare me." She spun around and stomped up onto the porch. Before she looked in the window, she turned back around and said, "Just because I'm a girl, don't get the idea that you can fool me." And she turned back and peered in the window.

Peter nudged me and whispered, "I give her ten seconds. She'll be running down here screaming her head off."

Ashley kept looking.

"See it?" I asked. "The body?"

No answer.

"It's right over there near the fireplace," Peter said.

Still no answer.

"Maybe she's too scared to move," I said to Peter. "Let's go see."

We walked slowly up to the front porch and stood next to Ashley.

"What's the matter, Ashley?" I asked. "You too scared to talk?"

"No. I'm not scared. I'm not sure it's a body. It looks like a body, but it's so dark in there, it's hard to tell. I think we should try to get a closer look."

That Ashley. Who could figure her? Peter and I couldn't wait to get out of there, and Ashley wanted to snoop around.

"Let's go," said Peter. "It's none of our business."

"If that's a woman in there," said Ashley, "she might be hurt. Maybe she fainted. Maybe she needs help."

"Maybe she's dead," I added. "Then what?"

"Then we leave," said Peter. "Ashley's right. Let's try to get in the cabin and look around. Let's go around back. Maybe there's a window open that we could climb into."

Ashley walked over to the front door. "Let's try the door. Maybe it's open."

"Don't be silly," I said. "The cabin's all closed up. Nobody's going to leave the front door open."

Ashley pushed on the old-fashioned latch and the door squeaked open. She must have been as surprised as we were, because she stepped back and said, "See? It's open. Now you guys can go ahead in and take a look around."

"Us guys? *Us?*" My voice practically squeaked. "This was your idea. *You* go look around."

"Why? You scared?"

48

That was too much for Peter. "Well, I'm not scared." He stopped at the open door and stuck his head in. "Just cautious." He took a step into the dark cabin with me and Ashley right behind.

"Do you see her?" I whispered.

"Over there," Peter whispered back, pointing into the corner. We took another step toward the heap in the corner and stopped. "She's wearing gloves," he said. "But I can't see her face. She's got so many clothes on, and that bonnet is hiding her head."

"Go look," Ashley whispered loudly and gave me a shove that threw me off balance. I collided with Peter and the two of us landed on the floor, a few feet from the collapsed woman. I closed my eyes, not wanting to see anyone who was dead.

Peter jumped up and, as I opened my eyes, he said, "Look at this. It's not a body. It's a whole heap of women's clothes, with skirts and shawls and a hat and gloves. The way it's heaped up, in the dark and all, it looks just like a body."

Ashley and I went over to where he was going through the clothes. "And look at these old lanterns," she said. "I wonder who left this stuff here. I'll bet it's been here for a hundred years."

I walked over to the fireplace. "No, it hasn't. Someone's been here—recently. They must have been burning some papers." I reached down and pulled out a half-burned, folded sheet of paper. I opened it carefully and saw some scratchy writing on it. The paper was sooty and a lot of it was burned, but I could make out a few of the words that were left. As I read those words, I could feel something like ice forming in the pit of my stomach.

49

Peter came over. "What's that, Murphy?"

"I don't know. But look at this," I said, flattening out the crumpled note on the table.

Peter traced the words with his finger and read aloud, ". . . a menace . . . too old . . . must act quickly." One sentence was complete at the bottom of the sheet: "As a last resort, eliminate the three sisters."

Ashley gasped. "What did you say?"

"Here, look for yourself," Peter said. "Murphy found this half-burned note in the fireplace. Someone wants to eliminate the three sisters."

"Who would want to hurt those sweet sisters?" Ashley asked with horror in her voice.

Peter laughed. "Sweet?"

Ashley glared at him. "They *are* sweet. And it sounds like someone wants to kill them."

"Let's not jump to conclusions," I said. "That's the kind of thing that only happens in the movies."

"Oh, yeah? Then how would you interpret that note, Mr. Know-It-All?" Ashley asked. "That's a death threat if I ever read one. We'll have to warn them."

"You're right," said Peter. "Hang onto that piece of paper, Murphy. It's our proof."

All of a sudden we heard a rumbling outside. Ashley ran to the window and peered through a crack. "Someone's coming. In a pickup truck. We'd better get out of here. Maybe it's the murderers."

We ran toward the back of the cabin. "Hurry," Peter shouted. "Let's get out the back door." He grabbed the handle and shoved. Then he pushed his body against it. "Oh no, it's jammed shut."

Chapter

ELEVEN

Ashley's voice was almost a shriek. "I hear the truck door slamming. Do something. We're going to get caught."

I looked around desperately, saw a wooden door with a latch on it, and opened it. "Quick. In here. It looks like a closet." The three of us scrambled in and pulled the door shut. It was pitch black and smelled musty, but it was better than getting caught out in the open by some lunatic.

We heard the front door creak open and a man's voice mutter, "Dang, I knew we forgot to lock that door." Another voice answered, but it was too muffled to hear what was said. We heard shuffling. Then the man said, "Better put this stuff back in the closet. I don't like it laying around here like this."

Ashley sucked in her breath, and I could feel myself break into a sweat. I didn't know how many people were out there, but I'd fight them all to the death, if I had to. I was just hoping I wouldn't have to.

Peter whispered in my ear, "If they open this door, don't ask questions, just run as fast as you can. It's every man for himself."

Ashley let out a little squeak and Peter whispered, "Girls, too, Ashley. Just run like your life depends on it."

Time stood still. I strained to hear every little noise, every creak and thump on the floor, every muttered word. The footsteps came closer. I could feel Ashley's and Peter's hot breath on my neck. I reached out in the dark, ready to shove and run, when my hand felt a long, cold door handle. I grabbed it with both hands and held on tight. I could feel someone pull. I held my breath and held on tighter.

"Dang door's stuck again," the man's voice said. "Must be warped with the damp and cold." And suddenly the pressure on the handle stopped. He spoke again. "Just put that stuff in the old trunk. I'll have to get my tools and plane the door down. But I can't be bothered now. Come on. Let's get going before the fog rolls in. We've got work to do. Make sure you lock up this time."

I listened as the front door creaked open and then was slammed shut. I let out my breath in a big *whoosh*. I could hear Peter and Ashley taking big gulps of air behind me.

"Open the door, Murphy," Ashley gasped. "I'm about to suffocate." I pushed the door open and we all tumbled out.

"That was close," said Peter. "How come he couldn't get the door open?"

"He didn't try real hard," I answered, realizing that

one big pull on his side would have gotten the door open easily. "I was pulling it shut from the inside."

"I wonder who that was?" Ashley asked, obviously unimpressed by my heroics.

Peter and I walked back toward the fireplace. "I don't know. I think there were at least two of them."

"And one of them was Captain Albert Stark," said Peter.

"Are you sure?" I asked.

Peter bent down and picked something up. "No, but this looks like the package we delivered to him a little while ago. The name and address have been ripped off, but I think it's the same one."

Ashley came over. "Open it up. Let's see what's in it."

Peter pulled the cover off the long cardboard cylinder, reached in, and pulled out a roll of paper. He brought it over to the table and Ashley and I helped him unroll it. "It's another map. With those strange half-star marks handwritten on it. And down here he wrote something. What does it say?"

I bent over and squinted at the scrawls. "It looks like *Beacon* and *Twins*. And it's got February 25th written on it." I looked at the other two. "Anyone got any idea what that might mean?"

Ashley's face lit up. "It's the sisters. Remember? That's what Cecily called Abigail—The Beacon. Because she's the oldest and was their guide. And the twins—"

"Bernice and Cecily," said Peter. "And February 25th is the day after tomorrow. Murphy, where's that note you found in the fireplace? Compare the handwriting. Maybe we can tell if Albert wrote the note."

I looked around. The note. Where was it? In all the confusion it was gone. I started searching frantically and finally found it right inside the closet door. Ashley came over and took it.

"Hey. Give that back."

"I'll hang onto it. You'll just lose it again, and it's our only proof that someone wants to kill the sisters." She walked over to the table and laid the note down next to the map. "It looks like the same handwriting. At least I think it does." She studied the map and note. "It's Albert all right. I knew when we met him he was up to no good."

"Why would he want to hurt the sisters?" I asked.

Peter tapped his head. "Just like Abigail said, 'loneliness does strange things to people.' And I don't know of anyone lonelier or stranger than Captain Albert Stark. Come on, let's get out of here."

TWELVE

We hurried back to where our bikes were hidden.

"Give me the note, Ashley. I'll put it my pocket," I said.

"No, it's too fragile. I'll put it in the basket of my bike."

"That's a dumb idea," said Peter. "It'll blow away. Give it to me. I'll carry it."

But Ashley insisted. She found a good-sized rock, brushed the sand off it, and put it on top of the note in her basket. "There. Now it won't blow away. If we lose this, we won't have any proof that someone wants to hurt the sisters. And I know that someone is Albert."

Peter looked around. "There must be another road out of this place."

"What makes you say that?" I asked.

"That truck sure didn't come through that path down by the cliff. Why don't we see if we can find it?"

"We might get lost," said Ashley. "We can come back another time and look around again."

We went back the way we had come. When we got to the part of the road that had washed away, I stopped. The incoming tide had almost reached the bottom of the cliff, and the surf thundered and boomed. I could barely hear Peter, who was last in line, urge me on.

"Go on, Murphy," he yelled.

I looked down at the angry surf below us.

"What are you waiting for?" Ashley asked, giving my bike a bump with hers.

I took a deep breath. Slowly I pushed the bike onto the narrow sand path. I made sure not to look down, but I couldn't block out the sound of the crashing surf.

I was almost at the other side when I heard Ashley shriek, "My bike—it's sliding."

I shoved my bike into the brambles and turned around. As if in slow motion, the ground beneath Ashley's bike began to crumble and slide down the cliff. The wheel caught on a root that was jutting out of the sand, but the rock in her basket tumbled out and the note hung for a moment in the air. Peter yelled, "Ashley, don't—" as she reached for the note, lost her balance, and went tumbling down the cliff.

Peter and I stood together, looking down in horror at the limp form of Ashley far below.

We pulled up her bike and shoved it into the brambles with ours, then sat at the edge of the cliff and pushed off. Tons of sand started sliding along with me, so I closed my eyes tight and wrapped my arms around my head, hoping I wouldn't collide with scraggly tree roots or sharp rocks.

Peter was right behind me, and we came to a stop a few feet from Ashley, still lying lifeless where she had landed.

We hurried over to her. "Ashley? Are you all right?"

She groaned, rolled over on her back, and slowly sat up. "I think so." She brushed the sand from her face and hair.

"What happened?" I asked. "How did you fall?"

She looked at me, then at Peter, as if trying to remember something that had happened a long time ago. "The note," she said finally. "My bike started to slide and the note was right there in front of me when I reached for it. Where is it? And where's my bike?"

"Forget the note," Peter said. "It's gone. Your bike's up on top with ours. Let's see if we can climb back up."

Our sliding had caused a minor avalanche of sand so that the cliff was almost straight up and down with the top of it sticking out farther than the bottom. Trying to climb only brought more sand down on top of us.

We were stuck on a narrow ledge of sand. On one side of us was the cliff; on the other, the ocean, not more than a few feet away, roaring closer and closer as each wave crashed.

"Any suggestions?" Peter asked.

"Let's walk along the bottom and see if we can find someplace that's not so steep. Then maybe we can climb back up," I said.

The ocean spray was throwing up a film of water, so we couldn't see more than a few feet in front of us. I was the last in line as we went single file on the sandy ledge, and as we walked, the sand crumbled behind us. I knew we'd never be able to come back this way.

We trudged on about a hundred feet when Peter stopped. We saw wooden stairs with a railing, but the bottom part had been washed away and, because the cliff behind them had been eroded, the rest of them were dangling in the air.

"They don't look safe," said Ashley.

"We don't have many other choices," Peter answered. "Come on, Ashley. We'll give you a boost up first."

The bottom step hung about a foot over our heads.

Peter and I locked our hands together to make a platform and Ashley stepped on them and we boosted her up. Grabbing the railing, she lifted herself onto the stairs. "Go to the top," I shouted. "I don't think it will hold all three of us at the same time." She scrambled up.

"Go ahead. You next," I said as I locked my hands together for Peter to step on.

He hesitated. "But what about you? How are you going to get up?"

"I have a plan. Go on. Hurry up." I gave him a boost and he grabbed the railing.

When he was at the top, I jumped up and grabbed the bottom step. I began to pull myself up. Suddenly, without warning, the step broke and sent me tumbling back into the sand.

Ashley, lying on her stomach and looking over the edge, hollered, "Hurry up. The tide must be coming in."

Sure enough. A wave boomed and the surf hissed up a few inches from me. The next wave brought water to my feet. I crawled hurriedly back to where the steps hung above me, the broken step dangling. I grabbed the broken piece, pulled myself up, and started up the steps. They were swaying with my weight and, as I looked down, I saw a wave wash under me and eat away another small chunk of the cliff.

"Hurry up," Ashley called. She and Peter were flat on their stomachs, reaching for me.

Suddenly I heard a cracking sound. Then another wave boomed and I felt the spray of the surf. Just as I reached for the top step, a huge wave smashed against the cliff, hitting the bottom of the stairs. They trembled and collapsed beneath me.

Chapter

THIRTEEN

I started to fall. Ashley and Peter reached out and each one grabbed me under an arm. There I was, dangling in mid-air as the steps were pulled away by the waves.

I shut my eyes, not wanting to see the drop beneath me. Slowly, slowly, Ashley and Peter hoisted me up.

We lay panting at the top, watching the surf crash against the cliff, watching the steps splinter and wash out to sea, watching the place we had stood a few minutes before covered by the angry surf.

I smiled at Peter and Ashley. "Thanks, guys."

"We'd better get the bikes and get back," Peter said. "I don't know about you, but I'm freezing—and hungry."

We got our bikes and rode to the inn. My hands were so cold I thought they'd freeze to the handlebars and even my heavy jacket didn't keep out the wind. I was almost looking forward to a bowl of Abigail's soup.

When we walked in the front door, we could hear voices arguing in the kitchen.

"We'll never change our minds," Abigail was saying. "And don't think that your threats can frighten us, Mr. Killeran."

A young man in some kind of brown uniform was sitting at the table. He had a thin, bony face and small brown eyes. "It wasn't a threat," he said. He was talking quietly, but he was pulling at his collar and his face was turning red, so I knew he was angry, too.

She shook a fist at him and raised her voice a little more. "Single-minded, that's what you are. You don't think about the people whose lives you'll be disrupting. All you think about is making a name for yourself with your fancy projects. Like those old lighthouses. Wasting money on old places. People around here say they're haunted."

"That's nonsense," Killeran said gruffly. "I'll admit that something strange is going on, but I'll get to the bottom of it. Those lighthouses are my pet project and nothing will stand in my way." He gave a little laugh. "Not even ghosts."

Abigail stood and walked over to him. "Better watch your step, Mr. Killeran. No man is a match for the spirit world. This part of the Cape has been undisturbed by progress for many years. And no one should be allowed to spoil it."

We walked into the kitchen. The man looked at us, then back at Abigail, and said, "This conversation is going nowhere." He put on his broad-brimmed hat, which was a little too big and rested lightly on his ears, zipped up his heavy brown jacket, and turned to leave. "Think it over. I'll be back. You may change your minds yet."

"Never," was Abigail's answer.

After he had left, Abigail sat down again, her hands shaking.

"Who was that?" Ashley asked.

"A government man—a ranger," Abigail said, shaking her head. "Making threats, wanting to turn our house into some kind of fancy museum." She looked up and I guess she suddenly realized that she was talking to three kids. "Nothing to worry about," she said quickly. Then, changing the subject, "You look cold. There's soup on the stove. Help yourselves." And she walked out of the room.

Peter looked at me. "Do you think the government would actually make threats against three old women?"

"I doubt it," I said. "But who knows? Everyone around here seems a little crazy."

"What about the death threat we found?" Ashley asked. "Should we mention something to the sisters? Tell them they're in danger? Or tell our moms?"

I thought about it. "I don't think so," I finally said. "Who would believe us, especially without proof?"

That night, as Peter and I climbed into bed, he said, "Maybe we can look for some more clues tomorrow." And he turned out the light.

I must have fallen asleep. I was dreaming about strange lights and falling off cliffs when my eyes snapped open and I looked into gloomy gray, the first light of early morning. I could see the dim outline of Peter, still fast asleep. Why was I awake? Then I heard something outside.

I ran to the window, but the morning fog was so thick it was like staring into white paste. A light shimmered somewhere below me. Four shadowy figures carrying flickering lights appeared and disappeared in the fog.

I went over and shook Peter. "Hurry up," I whispered loudly. "You've got to wake up and see this."

He opened one eye, propped himself up on one elbow, and grunted, "What time is it?"

"Never mind. Just get up. There are people out there . . . or ghosts . . . something . . ."

He looked mad. "You and your nightmares."

I pulled him out of bed. "No, honest. Hurry up." I dragged him to the window.

We looked out into empty fog. Peter said nothing, turned around, and started to trudge back to bed, but I grabbed him again. "I know what I saw. I'll prove it to you."

"How?"

"The widow's walk. We can see all around us. Come on." Peter was behind me as I opened the door and started up the iron staircase. The steps creaked slightly and I hoped they would hold our weight, but I had to prove to Peter that it wasn't my imagination.

At the top of the stairs I pushed against the hatch door. It thumped open and we pulled ourselves onto the roof.

Peter shuddered. "It's cold up here. And I can't see anything with all this fog."

I strained my eyes and looked around. About fifty feet behind the house lights flickered. I spun Peter around. "There," I whispered hoarsely. "See them?" .

"I sure do," Peter said, suddenly wide awake. The fog separated and we watched as four shadowy figures drifted into a fenced-in area. And then, without warning, they were gone. It was as if the air had swallowed them up without a trace. And then the fog closed in again and we couldn't even see the gate.

Peter and I just stared at each other. "Wh-where did they go?" he stuttered.

I was so scared I couldn't answer.

A loud screech tore through the air. I sucked in my breath. "Raccoons?" I gasped, hoping Peter would say yes.

But he just stared at me, his hair practically standing on end. "I wouldn't bet on it. Let's get out of here," he said, and the two of us clattered back down the rickety stairs, letting the hatch slam shut behind us.

Chapter

FOURTEEN

We stayed awake talking, waiting for the sun to come up so we could go outside and look around. But the fog turned to drizzle and the drizzle to a cold rain that beat on the windows and made the day dark.

As we went down to breakfast with Ashley trailing a few feet behind us, I said, "We've got to find out what's going on."

"What are you talking about?" Ashley asked.

I told her about the shadowy figures we had seen and the scream we had heard.

She stopped in the middle of the staircase and started to laugh. "You're a riot. First it's a body of an old lady and now it's ghosts. What an imagination."

"We're not imagining things," Peter said. "Something's going on. I think it has something to do with what we found in the cabin. Someone's after the sisters, and that could put all of us in danger."

Ashley shook her head and muttered, "Boys! And they say girls are dramatic. Give me a break."

Only Cecily was in the kitchen. "Hi, kids. Isn't this rain terrible? I found a puzzle you might like to work on later. And I'm in charge of breakfast. Ready for some cereal?"

The thought of another morning of Sugar Shocks sent chills to my jaw. I walked over to the stove and stirred the gook in the pot. The thought of Abigail's oatmeal made my throat tighten.

"What's the chance of having toast with some peanut butter and jelly?" I asked.

"Sure," Cecily said and went to the cupboard. "Here's the bread . . . and the peanut butter . . . and the —" She turned around, holding a small jar. "—and the jelly's empty. Oh dear. It looks like we'll have to have cereal after all."

"Maybe there's another jar of jelly around somewhere," I suggested.

She thought for a minute. "There is a jelly pantry. And lots of jelly. But it's down in the cellar, and I don't like to go down there."

"Why not?" Peter asked.

She looked around, leaned forward, and said in a dramatic whisper, "*Ghosts.*" She drew in her breath and stared at us, looking scared. "The cellar was once an old pirate cave where they tortured people. Now it's haunted."

Peter gave a low whistle.

My jaw dropped. "You're kidding."

Suddenly Cecily broke into a grin and started to giggle. "Had you going there, didn't I?"

"You *are* kidding," Ashley said. "You're a great actress."

"I don't know about 'great,' " Cecily said. "I was

on the stage for over thirty years. Now our guests are my audience, and I sill love acting. But let me run down-stairs and get the jelly."

"I'll go with you," Ashley said.

Cecily smiled. "Okay. But we'll need a flashlight. This part of the cellar is actually very small, but the lights have been out for years. The jelly pantry's right at the foot of the stairs."

Cecily found a flashlight, opened the cellar door, and beckoned Ashley to follow her. They disappeared into the dark. I practically held my breath waiting for them, but in just a few minutes they were back, with a tiny jar of jelly.

Cecily sat down with us, and as I reached for a piece of toast, I asked, "I was just wondering. If Abigail doesn't like tourists so much, how come you rent out rooms all summer?"

"It's for the money," Cecily said. "We inherited this house—we all grew up here, you know—but it's big and very expensive. The Beacon—Abigail, I mean—decided that renting the rooms would help pay the bills. But you're right, she doesn't like it."

She suddenly looked at the large watch she was wear-ing and said, "Oh dear, oh dear, I'm late, I'm late."

Ashley giggled. "Now you sound just like the white rabbit in *Alice in Wonderland*. What are you late for?"

"A meeting," she said, standing up. "I did once play the Queen of Hearts in *Alice*. It was my favorite part. I got to boss everyone around and say 'Off with his head, off with his head,' " and she chopped at the air.

"What meeting?" Ashley asked. But Cecily had al-ready left.

Peter laughed. "Weird," he said.

"But nice," Ashley added. "It's exciting knowing a real actress."

"Right," I said. "But are you sure we didn't drop down some rabbit hole?"

We sat munching on the rest of our toast. "This jelly is pretty good," I said. "It must be homemade. Wonder what they put in it?"

"Maybe arsenic," Peter suggested. "I saw this movie once about an old woman who was slowly poisoning some guests who wouldn't leave. She put poison in all the sweet stuff, like jelly." He scraped the little jar and put a blob on his toast.

"You and your movies," I said, putting my toast back on my plate.

It was still raining after we cleaned up, so we started the old lighthouse puzzle Cecily had left for us.

After about an hour I stood up, stretched, and said, "This is boring. Why don't we go outside or something."

"It's pouring," said Ashley. "Come on. Help me finish."

But Peter was getting bored, too. He stretched out on the floor for a minute then sat up abruptly. "Listen."

I listened. "What? I don't hear anything except the rain."

"That's what I mean. It's so quiet. Where are the sisters?"

Peter and I walked quietly into the kitchen—empty. We looked into a few other rooms—a dining room, a pantry, a sun porch—no one. "Come on," said Peter. "Let's explore the house."

"Maybe they're sleeping," I said.

"Or at some meeting," Peter said. "But that's okay.

67

Their rooms are all at the other side of the house on the second floor. Let's look around the third floor."

"What about Ashley?"

"We'll leave her with the puzzle," he said, starting up the stairs.

No such luck. "Where are you going?" Ashley asked, coming up behind us.

"We're just going to look around. Go back to your puzzle, Ashley."

"I'd rather come with you."

We went up to the third floor and looked into all of the rooms. They were bedrooms, closed up for the winter with the shades drawn and sheets pulled over the furniture. At the end of the hall we opened another door and discovered a narrow, low passageway with three steps at the end. It smelled musty and damp. A little bit of dusty light filtered down from somewhere.

"Let's see where this goes," suggested Peter.

Ashley took a step back. "Let's not. It smells old and we'll get all dirty."

"Then you stay here," I said, ducking down and leading the way.

But of course she didn't.

_____ **Chapter** _____

FIFTEEN

At the top of the stairs was a huge, unfinished room that looked like an attic. Furniture, pictures, boxes, and trunks, all covered with dust, had been stored in there with racks of old clothes and hatboxes—dozens of hatboxes. Weedy-looking bunches of dried stuff hung from the beams along with delicate loops of spider webs.

Ashley, ignoring the dust and the spiders, ran for the hatboxes, opened one, and pulled out a wide-brimmed red hat with a droopy purple feather. "I love it," she squealed, putting on the hat and admiring herself in a dusty mirror. She stuffed it back into the box, opened another, and pulled out a yellow hat draped with faded yellow gauze.

Peter and I left Ashley posing and headed for the trunks. Peter started to lift the lid on one of them.

I pushed it back down. "I'm not sure we should do this. What if there's a body in there?"

He looked at me and smiled. "This isn't Albert's attic, you know."

"I know. But the sisters aren't exactly what you'd call normal senior citizens. Maybe we'll find some tourists who didn't pay their bills."

Peter gave a Dracula chuckle. "Maybe we will." And he opened the trunk.

No body, just dusty clothes. Another trunk was filled with papers. He looked through some of them and said, "More old maps."

"And a couple of old pictures," I said, picking up two pictures that had fluttered to the floor.

The pictures were of people standing near a short, squat lighthouse. One was of three teenage girls in old-fashioned clothes. Two of them were twins with their arms around each other, laughing. The third girl looked more serious. In the other picture a young man and one of the girls were standing next to the lighthouse. The girl looked like one of the twins, but it was hard to tell because the lighthouse took up most of the picture.

I showed Peter. "The girls in these pictures must be the sisters," I said. "Wonder who the guy is?"

He looked at the backs of the pictures. "There's writing on them. This one of the girls says 'A, B, C.' The other one says 'The Beacon.' " We turned that picture back over and looked at it again. "You think that's Abigail? The Beacon? It looks more like one of the twins. Whoever took the picture should have gotten closer. There's too much lighthouse."

We were puzzling over the pictures when Ashley called. "Murphy. Peter. Where are you? Look what I found."

We went back to where we had left Ashley. She was sitting on the floor surrounded by hatboxes and was wearing a black feathered hat with a veil draped over her eyes and nose. "Nice hat," I said. "That's what you called us over to see?"

"No. Look what I found in one of the hatboxes. Letters—about twenty of them—tied with a dark red velvet ribbon. They're love letters. Or at least most of them are." The black veil was fluttering near her mouth as she talked, and she kept puffing at it.

"Love letters? Who cares about old love letters?" I said. "Besides, you shouldn't be reading someone else's letters."

"I know," she said. "But maybe they can help us figure out what's going on. The first couple were written to Cecily. All the rest are to Bernice. They're not signed, but they're all in the same handwriting and I know they're from a man."

I picked up one of the letters. "Yuck! Listen to this mush. 'You are my light, my life. Without you I am nothing.' " I looked at Ashley. "This is a clue?"

Ashley started to say something, but Peter started reading another letter, making his voice all sappy and dramatic. " 'You are so different from the other. I thought I loved her, but I was wrong. Even though you look like her, I could tell right away. No one will ever keep us apart.' " I thought we were going to fall over from laughing.

Ashley just sat on the floor, holding one last letter, and giving us her Miss-Mature look. "Before you bust from laughter, you'd better read this one." She handed me the letter she had been holding.

It was shorter than the others, just a lot of choppy phrases, dated February, but also with no year. I started reading aloud, ready for another good laugh. " 'I have had enough. Your tricks. Or hers. It doesn't

71

matter. Someday I shall have my revenge. On both of you. On all of you. It may take me a hundred years, but you will be sorry. No one makes a fool of me.' "

It was, like the others, unsigned.

"Who do you think wrote it, Peter?"

He took the letter and examined it closely. Then he looked at me. "The handwriting looks like Albert's. I recognize it from the maps and from the note."

"So it's from Albert," Ashley said, stuffing the hat back into the hatbox. "So what does that mean?"

I put the letters, except the last one, back. "So it means that Albert is after the sisters. Something must have happened a long time ago. Cecily started talking about Albert at breakfast yesterday and Bernice spilled the milk."

Ashley nodded and said, "He must have been in love with one of them but something went wrong. Bernice moved away and got married. Albert probably waited all this time, and now that Bernice is back, he's ready to get his revenge."

Peter added, "And according to the note we found in the old cabin, he's probably planning to get it this week—to eliminate the sisters."

Ashley sucked in her breath. "You're right. Of course. A case of love gone bad. He must have been brooding over this for a long time. Now he wants to get revenge. We've got to do something. To save them."

I looked at the picture I had found, the one that said "The Beacon" on the back. "So where does Abigail fit in? Is this her with Albert?"

Peter put a hand on my shoulder and said, "Shhh. I heard something. Let's get out of here before someone finds us. Take that letter with you—we'll put it back later, before anyone misses it."

"Right," I said, putting it in my pocket along with the pictures.

We went quietly down the three stairs, through the passage, and out the door. Just as we closed it, Bernice appeared out of nowhere. She looked at us, at the door behind us, and pulled her gray shawl closer around her. "Where are you coming from?" she asked.

"Our rooms," I said quickly. "But we took a wrong turn somewhere and we've been looking for the stairs."

That seemed to satisfy her. "Just don't go snooping around," she said in almost a whisper. "It makes Abigail nervous. Come on. I'll show you the way down."

As she turned to go, she reached out for the doorknob behind us, testing if it was locked. When the door opened, she let out a breathless little gasp and quickly shut the door, as if afraid something from behind it might escape. She reached in her pocket and pulled out a key.

Locking the door, she said, "Old memories should be forgotten."

"How long have you known Albert?" Ashley asked. One thing about Ashley, no one could accuse her of being subtle.

Bernice pulled herself up taller and gripped her shawl. She got a tight, puckery look on her face. "Abigail will wonder where I am. Follow me if you want to find your way down." And she turned and marched silently ahead.

"Guess I hit a nerve," said Ashley.

"Guess you did," said Peter.

73

Chapter

SIXTEEN

Let's take a bike ride," I said after lunch. "It's not raining anymore and maybe we can get some clues to the lights I told you I saw on the beach."

Even though the rain had stopped, a gray mist hung in the air. The trees dripped water and everything smelled soggy and damp.

We biked down the road toward the beach. The rain must have riled up the ocean because we could hear great rushing waves and rumbling surf.

Near the cliff above the beach a man was standing by a pickup truck, the same man who had argued with Abigail in her kitchen.

"Hi, kids." He waved to us. "Kind of wet to be biking, isn't it?"

We pulled up near him and said "Hi."

"My name's James Killeran," he said and cocked his hat at an angle. "I'm a ranger with the National Seashore Park. I'm checking for any new erosion caused by the storm. We've been losing about three feet of beach a year to the ocean. Winter storms are always the worst."

He looked awfully young to be a ranger, but he seemed like a nice guy. He asked our names, and after we introduced ourselves he asked where we were from.

"Connecticut," I said. "We're staying at the inn for a few days."

Ashley was all excited. "You're a real ranger? That's neat. I'm in the gifted group at school and even though this is vacation, I'd like to do a report on the seashore. How come you're here now? Don't they close the park down for the winter?"

He smiled. "The National Seashore isn't exactly a park. It's land that the government owns and protects. Most of the Seashore here on the Cape is undeveloped. It's our job to see that its 27,000 acres remain un-spoiled. We're kind of policemen of the land."

"But there's nothing to police now," said Ashley.

"I'm in charge of restoring some historic buildings. It's my first assignment and it's very important to me. Right now I'm working on some old lighthouses. I'm researching their history and I want to see if I can get them into the National Register of Historic Places."

It started to drizzle again. Killeran walked toward his truck. "You kids better get back before it starts to rain again. Any time you want to talk more about the Sea-shore, come visit. I live down the road that way." He pointed to the road that ran parallel with the ocean. "Look for a path about a hundred yards down. It's a shortcut that'll take you right behind my cottage."

When we got back to the inn, the sky had cleared again. As we parked the bikes, Ashley said, "Why don't you and Peter show me where you said you saw those figures disappear."

"You mean you really believe us?" I asked, acting extremely shocked.

"I didn't say that. I just want to see where you're talking about."

We went out back and waded through a field of knee-high dry grass and brown weeds.

"There's the spot," Peter said, and started to run. Ashley and I ran after him.

Peter stopped, and when Ashley and I caught up with him, we were all out of breath.

At first no one said a word. We stood staring at a small graveyard that was surrounded by an iron fence, the tombstones almost overgrown by grass and weeds. As we stood and looked, a few wisps of fog began to swirl along the ground, and the sun ducked behind a cloud.

"Let's go in and look around," Ashley suggested.

"Why?" I asked. "You just said you wanted to see the place—well, this is it. Now let's go."

"No," said Peter, who looked almost hypnotized by the old graveyard. "This *is* where we saw those people disappear." Then he looked at me and said hoarsely, "Maybe they *were* ghosts."

The fog in the graveyard began to get thicker and I could feel prickles down the middle of my back. Looking at the old tombstones and thinking about the shadows that had disappeared in the early morning fog made me shiver.

Peter pushed open the rusty gate and walked in. Ashley followed and I walked in behind, as if something were guiding my steps. The old tombstones looked like slices of bread covered with green and golden mold. Some were leaning in odd positions; some had almost toppled over.

In the middle of the small cemetery one tombstone stood out. It was standing straight up and wasn't covered with the spotty mold or surrounded by weeds. Next to it was a small fallen statue of an angel with the head broken off.

Peter leaned close to it and read the faint inscription aloud: "IN MEMORY OF SARA ANN SNOW DIED FEBRUARY 25, 17—, I can't read the year; it's worn off."

Ashley gasped. "Sara Ann Snow? That's the girl who drowned in Abigail's story."

I was clammy all over and my legs wobbled like rubber bands. The fog, feeling like wet slime, began to surround us. We had to get out of there. I said in a whisper, "It's getting cold and it's going to start raining again. What do you say we—"

Peter cut me off. "Shhhh. I hear something."

By this time everything around us had become a gray blur. I strained to see through the fog, but could only make out moving points of light.

"What is it?" Ashley whispered.

"I don't know," Peter whispered back. "Lights—and voices. Coming this way."

We ran to the corner of the cemetery and crouched down behind a couple of moldy tombstones. The lights came closer and I could barely make out four shadowy forms. Their clothes seemed to float around them, and I couldn't tell if they were walking on solid ground or gliding a few feet above it.

Ashley, who had been hiding behind a tombstone right next to mine, made a quick move and ducked down behind me. "Who is it?" she whispered. "Or *what?*

"The same figures we saw this morning. Shhh. They'll hear you."

The shadows moved through the open gate. Eerie, echoing voices floated over to us through the fog. "Time's getting short . . . we have to act soon . . ."

"Do you hear that?" Ashley whispered in my ear.

"Shh," I whispered back, mad because I had missed what they said next.

Then I heard ". . . three sisters . . . we'll have to use the dynamite . . ." They seemed to be near the middle of the cemetery. I heard a grunt followed by a loud creak. Then it was silent, so silent that I could practically hear the fog curl around my ears. I didn't move and neither did Ashley. It was as if we had both turned to stone.

Finally we saw Peter's shadowy figure come toward us. "They're gone," he said. "Vanished. Just like the last time."

"Ghosts," was all Ashley could say.

"Then it's ghosts that are after the sisters," I said. "That's what they seemed to be talking about." I walked over to Sara Ann Snow's tombstone. "What do you think? Is it possible? I mean mooncussers, and ghosts, and that story about Sara Ann. I thought Abigail made it all up."

"Look at the date on the tombstone," said Ashley, tracing the stone with her finger. "February 25. That's tomorrow."

"It sure is," said Peter. "The date that Sara Ann's brother died and she washed out to sea. But why would ghosts be after the sisters?"

"Who knows," I said. "But it's time we stopped fooling around and told someone."

"Let's tell that ranger—James Killeran," Ashley said. "He probably knows the area better than anyone else. He'll know what to do. He's practically a policeman."

"Good idea," said Peter. "First thing in the morning. I'm not sure you two have noticed, but it's raining again, and it's getting dark."

I hadn't noticed. The three of us were standing there, in the middle of a dark cemetery, in the pouring rain. "Let's get back," I said. "Before the sisters send a search party for us."

Chapter

SEVENTEEN

I didn't sleep well that night. I dreamed of ghosts floating and disappearing, Abigail dressed like a witch stirring an iron cauldron, mooncussers walking the beach carrying lanterns, Albert Stark digging graves. Then they all got together and started chasing me, and I was running toward a short, fat lighthouse like the one we saw in the picture we found in the attic. But I was running on the sand and my feet wouldn't move and they were getting closer and closer when suddenly, out of nowhere, James Killeran came riding up in his truck and saved me. When I woke up, I knew he was the answer to our problems.

It was a beautiful, sunshiny morning. We all rushed through breakfast and then politely excused ourselves. As we got our bikes, Ashley asked, "Did you bring that letter and the pictures? The ones from the attic? We should show them to Mr. Killeran."

I patted my back pocket. "Right here."

"Good," she said. "I know you won't lose them."

And she wasn't being snotty. It was as if our whole problem of trying to figure out how to save the sisters was bringing us all a little closer.

It was easy finding the path to Killeran's, but because the sand was so loose, we couldn't ride our bikes.

"Let's leave them here by the road," Peter suggested. "His cottage can't be too far. I can see the roof over that sand dune."

As we walked toward the back of the cottage, we could hear voices. Two men were talking, loud and angry, somewhere in front of the house. We were just ready to walk around the cottage when we heard, "—the three sisters. They're more trouble than they're worth—" Then the voice faded.

We stopped and looked at each other. Peter put a finger to his lips. "Shhh." We sneaked around to the side of the cottage to try to hear more.

I recognized Killeran's voice. "I don't know what to do," he said.

"Well, I'll tell you this much," the other man said. "The workmen won't put up with much more. We drop off supplies, and then the nails are missing. Then they're back and something else is gone. If I didn't know better, I might almost believe that they *are* haunted."

"Any vandalism?" Killeran asked.

"Not really," the man said. "But it's frustrating and we're way behind schedule. Who's going to pay all the overtime?"

"I'm under real pressure," Killeran said. "This whole thing could get us a promotion—and a raise. But if it doesn't get done by summer, we could both be out of a job."

It was quiet for a minute. Then the man said, "And

those women who own the inn? Did you see them again?''

Killeran's voice sounded even angrier. "They're a detriment to progress. A problem that has to be eliminated. But don't worry. I have a plan."

"I sure hope so," the man said. "The situation is getting desperate. I'd better get back and see what else has happened." A few minutes later we heard a car drive off.

Peter, Ashley, and I looked at each other in shock. Peter motioned us to the back of the cottage and we huddled down. "Did you hear that?" I whispered. "It must be Killeran. He must be the one who's behind everything."

"I don't believe it," Ashley whispered. "He seemed so nice. Why would he want to hurt the sisters?"

"You heard him," Peter said. "Because they're standing in his way. And you've got to stop thinking everyone's so nice, Ashley."

"We'd better get out of here," Ashley said. "Before Killeran finds us and eliminates us."

Peter stood up. "I've got a better idea," and he started to walk around to the front of the cottage.

"Where's he going?" Ashley asked.

"I don't know," I answered. "But we'd better go with him."

Killeran was standing in front of the cottage, frowning. When he saw us, he put on a smile—a big phony smile. "Hi, kids," he said. "Isn't this a beautiful day? Yesterday afternoon the fog was so bad we had to use flashlights. This morning the sky's so clear that I swear we could see across the Atlantic to Ireland." He pointed toward the ocean where the horizon of sea and water met in a deep blue line. "What can I do for you?"

"You mentioned something yesterday about information on the Seashore," Peter said. "Ashley's doing a report. Maybe you could help."

Killeran smiled. "Why don't you come inside and I'll see if I have some pamphlets for you. After you look them over, you can come back and we'll talk some more."

Ashley was frowning. "I don't think—"

"Great idea," interrupted Peter. "We'll all come in. We're all interested in Ashley's report, aren't we, Murphy?" And he turned toward me and winked.

"Sure," I said, hesitantly. "We definitely are interested in Ashley's report."

Killeran led the way with Ashley behind him. As we walked into the cottage, Peter whispered to me, "Keep your eyes open for anything that looks unusual."

"Right."

The cottage was small: a living room with two chairs and a television, an opening in the back wall that looked into a kitchen, a closed door to our right that was probably a bedroom. Most of the living room was filled with file cabinets and boxes, and Killeran started to look through them as soon as we got in.

Ashley walked over to us and whispered, "What's the big idea? The man's probably a killer, and you get us invited in."

"That's the whole point," I whispered back. "Now keep him occupied while Peter and I look around."

Ashley glared at us. "Oh, sure, I do all the dirty work while you have all the fun," she said, but she went over to where Killeran was crouched down over a box and

83

said sweetly, "I hope you can find a lot of stuff, Mr. Killeran. I want to do a really great report."

Peter and I strolled casually into the kitchen. It, too, was cluttered with boxes, most of them still sealed. I casually lifted the lid on one that wasn't, but it was filled with pots and pans. Another had newspaper clippings in it. One article dated a few weeks ago had the headline: KILLERAN TO ACT AS TEMPORARY HEAD OF CAPE'S HISTORIC BUILDINGS PROJECT.

In the article he was quoted as saying, "Nothing will stand in my way to preserve the history of the Cape." He must have liked that one, because he had about ten xerox copies of it. I looked around, saw that Ashley had Killeran occupied, folded a copy of the article, and put it in my pocket, which now contained the letter, the pictures, and the newspaper article. If I found much more stuff, I'd have to start carrying a briefcase.

"Pssst, Murphy, look at this." Peter was near the refrigerator, looking at something that was on the counter.

"What is it?" I asked, walking next to him.

"Maps. Look. Just like the ones we saw up in that other cottage. Same markings, same words."

I looked at what Peter was holding. The map looked identical to the one we had seen a few days ago. Same half-star markings, same words—"Beacon, Twin, Twin."

"And would you look at this," I said, opening the flap of a carton that was near our feet. It was labeled WARNING: HANDLE WITH CARE. KEEP AWAY FROM OPEN FLAME. Inside were long red sticks with fuses.

"Dynamite." Peter gasped. "It looks like a whole box of sticks of dynamite."

We took a step back. Suddenly Killeran's words broke through our concentration. "Boys?" He was looking through the opening in the wall. "Looking for something?"

Peter hurriedly dropped the map back on the counter and I shut the flap on the dynamite box. We turned around. "We just came in for a drink of water. If that's okay with you?"

He smiled his phony smile. "Sure. Help yourselves. There's some juice in the refrigerator."

Ashley had joined him at the opening. "Mr. Killeran has been most helpful. I have lots of information here. I want to get started on this report right away."

"Good idea, Ashley," Peter and I said almost at the same time. "We'd better get going," I added. "Maybe we can work some before lunch."

Killeran laughed. "I never saw kids so eager to do schoolwork. Isn't this vacation?"

"It's supposed to be, but it didn't seem to work out that way."

"Come again, kids," said Killeran as we were leaving. "Anytime. Have dinner with me. It gets lonely out here."

"And loneliness can do strange things to people," Ashley muttered as we left.

Chapter

EIGHTEEN

As we got our bikes, Ashley asked, "What did you find?"

"Not here," I said, looking around. "Let's find some place we can talk where we can be sure no one will hear us."

We biked a little way up and stopped near a stretch of sandy cliff overlooking the Atlantic. We parked our bikes and sat down.

No one said anything for a few seconds. The ocean was like blue glass covered with sun sparkles. One sea gull hovered above it, then dropped straight down and came back up with a fish in its bill. I could understand why the sisters didn't want anyone spoiling the beauty of this place.

"It's Killeran," Peter said flatly. "He must be the one who's behind all this."

"What did you find?" Ashley asked.

"Maps in the kitchen," Peter answered. "Just like the ones we saw in the cabin."

"But Albert had them, too. Remember?"

"I know," Peter said. "And I haven't figured it all out yet. But I'm sure Killeran's involved. There's more. Tell her, Murphy."

Ashley frowned. "You sure are being dramatic about all this. So you found maps. So what?"

"So we also found dynamite—a whole box of it. I'll bet he's going to use it on the sisters."

Ashley wasn't convinced. "How do you know it's dynamite? Have you ever seen any before?"

"No," Peter said. "But *everyone* knows what dynamite looks like—red sticks with long fuses."

"It was dynamite all right," I added.

Ashley thought for a while and said. "It doesn't make any sense. Why would he blow up their house when he wants it so badly for a museum?"

"I've already thought about that," Peter said. "He'll probably lure them away from the house to somewhere that's deserted—like maybe that old shack we found in the woods—and *ka-boooom*, suddenly his problems are all eliminated."

"You know, Peter, I never realized before how smart you are," Ashley said. "And did you catch what he said about the fog yesterday afternoon?"

We looked at her. "What do you mean?"

Her voice got real low. "He said the fog was so thick they had to use flashlights. Who did he mean by *they*? And how do we know *they* weren't the ones we saw in that old graveyard?"

"Good thinking, Ashley," Peter said.

All this admiration between Peter and Ashley was starting to get to me. "Okay, you two geniuses," I said.

"If it was Killeran, where did he disappear to? Are you sure we didn't see ghosts?"

"I'm not sure of anything," she answered. "Did you see anything else?"

"Nope," Peter said. "Just the maps and the dynamite."

"And this," I said, fishing the xerox copy of the article out of my back pocket. "This was in a box full of newspaper clippings. Look what Killeran says about nothing standing in his way."

"Then that explains his motive," Peter said. "He's looking for a promotion and he told that other guy that he was under a lot of pressure. He's our man. *Killer Killeran.*"

"I knew from the beginning he was no good," Ashley said.

I was about to point out to her that she was the one who suggested we get his help when she said, "He may work for the government, but he's a definite fanatic. He's young, and he wants a promotion, and he won't let anyone stand in his way."

"A real psycho," Peter murmured. "Now what?"

"I don't know," I said. "But we've got to think of something. Abigail and Bernice and Cecily may not be my favorite three people, but we can't let them get hurt."

"Or killed," Peter added. "Come on, let's ride around awhile. My brain needs a rest."

When we got back to the inn, we were all starved. No one seemed to be around, but Abigail's sludgy soup was bubbling on the stove. I picked up a ladle and stirred through the muck. "Sewer soup," I said, picking up a ladle full. I looked at it closely. "What are those lumps?"

Peter sniffed. "I don't know. But I'm not much in the mood for soup. I think I'll have a peanut butter and jelly sandwich."

"Yeah, me too," I said.

Ashley looked at the soup and then at the two of us. "I'll make them," she said. She started looking through all of the cupboards. "I can't find any jelly."

"We finished it," Peter said. "I scraped the last of it out of that little jar."

"That's okay," Ashley said, opening a drawer and pulling out a flashlight. "I'll get some more. I know right where it is."

"Want us to come?" I asked.

"No. I'll be right back," and she disappeared down the cellar steps.

We sat at the table. "Any ideas about Killeran?" I asked. "We're running out of time."

"I know."

We sat thinking. I could hear a clock ticking in the distance.

The quiet was suddenly pierced by a distant screech— the same screech we had heard before. "Racoons," I grumbled. "They sure can get on your nerves."

Another screech. Peter looked a little worried. "Do you think that was Ashley?" he asked.

"Ashley and raccoons have a lot in common," I said, and laughed at my clever joke.

But Peter didn't laugh. "She's been gone a long time."

"Maybe she's trying to decide on a flavor," I said.

We waited another minute. "Maybe we'd better go look for her," I suggested.

I walked over to the cellar steps and looked down. "It's dark," I whispered. "I can't see a thing." There were a few steps, then the landing, then the steps bent off to the right.

"Let's see if there's another flashlight around somewhere," he said.

We started looking through all the drawers and cupboards. "Find one?" I asked.

"No. But here's a candle and some matches. It'll have to do. We can't waste any more time looking for a flashlight. She's been gone too long."

He lit the candle and we started to walk slowly down the cellar steps. The candle didn't give much light. Shadows moved and a cobweb brushed against my face.

"Do you see anything?" I whispered as we turned the corner and I followed Peter down.

"Not yet. Where did she say the jelly pantry was?"

"Right at the bottom."

I felt as if I were walking in slow motion. The spooky cellar was the last place I wanted to be, but we had to find Ashley. We had joked about losing her, but this was no joke.

We reached the bottom and opened the door to the jelly pantry. Empty. We looked around. For such a big house, the cellar here was small. Nothing—no doors, no windows, no Ashley.

"Where *is* she?" I asked, annoyed that Ashley was putting us through this.

Suddenly another screech pierced the gloomy quiet, louder and shriller than any we had heard before. I gripped Peter's arm. Something creaked behind us. We whirled around fast. Too fast. The candle went out.

NINETEEN

I was afraid to move. Goosebumps were running down my arms and legs. "Peter?" I whispered hoarsely. Another creak.

"I'm looking for the matches," he whispered, his voice shaky.

Suddenly a light glowed on the landing of the steps. We were cornered, trapped. Ashley was gone and pretty soon we would be, too.

The light flickered around the corner and started down the steps. Someone was coming down with some kind of light.

"Hide," I whispered, pulling Peter behind the steps. We crouched down, trying to make ourselves invisible.

A dark figure, carrying an old lantern with a small flame fluttering in it, stopped at the bottom of the steps. It was so dark and shadowy, I couldn't tell if it was a man or a woman. The figure turned slowly, as if sensing we were there. I could hear Peter breathing next to me, and I was sure the mysterious figure could hear him, too. The light was too weak to reach us, but a few steps forward and we would be discovered.

The seconds dragged. The figure took another step toward us. Then it stopped, turned, and walked into the blackness. I heard a creak—a click—then nothing. Dark silence hung around us. We waited. Still nothing.

I stood up slowly. My muscles ached from the cramped position.

"Is it gone?" Peter whispered, still jammed against the wall.

"I think so."

"Let's not hang around to find out," he said. The two of us made our way up the stairs. We sat in the empty kitchen. I was sweaty and weak and scared. "We have to find Ashley. She must be in trouble."

"I'll bet Killeran has something to do with it," Peter said.

"Or Albert," I added. "Let's start with Albert's place—it's closer."

We walked over to Albert's through the woods, feeling like commandos on a mission. Killeran's truck was parked in Albert's driveway.

"What's *he* doing here?" I asked.

"They're in it together—Albert and Killeran," Peter answered.

We stayed behind bushes and shrubs as long as we could. When there was no more cover, we decided to crouch down low and head for the house.

We were practically crawling on our bellies when we got to the front window that had the big table near it. Peter put a finger to his lips. Even though the day was cool and the fog was beginning to drift in from the ocean, the window was a little open. We could hear voices from inside.

We had come in the middle of a conversation. Killeran was saying, ". . . tonight, but I don't know when. Probably late—depends on the weather."

Albert grunted a little and said, "Sounds good to me. But I'd like to see your plans. If you have no objection."

"That can be arranged," said Killeran. "I appreciate your cooperation. Take a ride with me now; I'll show you the spot I have planned."

"Should I take the map?" Albert asked.

"No need," Killeran replied. "I know the place by heart." And he laughed a sinister laugh.

Chairs scraped and we dashed for cover. We watched as Albert and Killeran got in Killeran's truck and drove away.

"What do you think?" Peter asked.

"Let's go inside and take a look around. Maybe they've got Ashley tied up in there."

We climbed in the window and rushed through every room in the small cottage. We even checked all the closets. No Ashley. But in one of the closets we found five sticks of dynamite in an old cardboard box.

"Will you look at this," Peter said. "Just like the stuff we saw at Killeran's. Now we know they're in on it together."

I wanted to get a closer look at the dynamite, but as I reached down to pick up a stick, Peter grabbed my arm. "Don't, Murphy. We don't know anything about dynamite. It might be dangerous. Right now we've got to find Ashley."

93

As we were about to crawl back out the window, Peter picked up a map and studied it.

"Is it the same as the others?" I asked.

"Not quite," he said. He spread it out on the table. "It has some new markings." He leaned close to the map. "Oh, no!"

"What? What?" I asked.

"There are three black X's marked in by hand. Each one is labeled. Someone wrote in black ink 'Beacon,' 'Twin,' 'Twin.' That must be where they're planning to bury the sisters. I told you Albert reminded me of that psycho in the movie, the one who killed people and marked their graves on a map."

"Is there a fourth X?" I asked.

"No, why?"

"I'm worried about Ashley."

TWENTY

By the time we got outside, the fog was as thick and dark as Abigail's sewer soup. Life was beginning to look more and more like Abigail's soup—lots of strange stuff floating around with no clue as to what was really there.

"Now what?" Peter asked. "Killeran's place?"

"I guess so. We've got to find Ashley, and I don't know where else to look."

"Let's get our bikes and go—before she becomes a new X on some old map."

We hurried to the back of the house where we had left our bikes. The fog was getting so heavy it seemed to hang from the tree branches like dirty curtains. We'd never find our way to Killeran's, but we had to try. I knew Ashley was in trouble.

A light flickered in the distance. Someone was near the old graveyard. We left the bikes and, using the fog and a few thick trees as cover, we worked our way closer. When we were almost at the graveyard, we jumped behind a tree. A shadowy figure, exactly like the one who had disappeared in the cellar, passed within a few feet of us.

"Should we follow it?" I whispered to Peter.

As the fog swallowed up the dark form, Peter grabbed my arm and pointed toward the graveyard. "Look. Another light." A thin beam of light, one that looked more like a flashlight than a lantern, pointed through the fog, first in one direction, then in another, then another. I looked back in the direction of the figure with the lantern.

"Come on," I said. "The phantom's gone. Let's see what the other light is—or who."

We circled wide, waited until the light was pointed away from us, crouched low, and moved in toward it. We were about a foot from whoever was holding the light when, without warning, the light spun around and shined right in our faces. Caught! Trapped! I stood frozen, wondering why I wasn't running away as fast as I could.

Suddenly I heard, "Murphy? Peter? Is that you?" Ashley! Standing with her flashlight in the middle of the graveyard.

My heart, pounding in my chest, calmed down. "What are you doing out here? We thought you were kidnapped when you went into the cellar. And how did you get away? And who just passed us in the fog?"

She sat on the ground, leaned against a tombstone, and shut off the flashlight. We sat in front of her. As she told her story, she became nothing more than a breathless voice floating through the fog.

"The jelly pantry—I reached up for the jar—my hand hit some kind of switch. All of a sudden there was a dark tunnel in front of me. I stepped inside—just to take a quick look around. But the opening slid shut and I was by myself on the other side. I tried to get it back open. But I couldn't. So I started down the tunnel."

She took a deep breath, shuddered, and continued. "The tunnel was disgusting—cement walls, dripping water, ugly smells. It had a few narrow passages branching off, but they were just dirt, so I stuck to the cement tunnel. Then I heard someone behind me. I didn't want to get caught, so I ducked into one of the dirt tunnels and hid. Somebody passed right near me—carrying a lantern and all dressed in black. But I couldn't tell who it was."

She stopped talking for a minute.

"And then what?" I asked.

"I followed whoever it was—I was so scared I'd get caught, but I had to find a way out. I watched as it went up some steps and through an opening, but it closed again. I watched awhile, climbed the steps, saw a lever and pulled. A hatch sprang open. I squeezed out. Then it shut again. And here I am." She turned on the flashlight. "But *where* am I?"

We stood up. I took her light and shined it on the tombstone she had been leaning against. "This is Sara Ann Snow's stone." I shined the light on the ground in front of it. The tall grass was all flat and matted. I kneeled down and felt the outline of a crack in the ground around it. "This tombstone—I think it's a fake. I'll bet it's the entrance to the tunnel."

"That's why this stone doesn't look as old and over-grown as the rest," said Peter.

"Maybe that's where those ghostly shadows disap-peared the other night," said Ashley. "But who was I following? Killeran or Albert?"

"Neither," I said. "They were both in Albert's cot-

97

tage and we saw them drive away." I looked at Ashley. "At least you're safe. Now let's figure out how to keep the sisters safe. We don't have much time. I think Albert and Killeran are out looking over the spot they plan to bury them in."

When we got back to the inn, Peter said, "We've got to do something. It's probably going to happen tonight. What time is it now?"

I looked at the clock on the mantel. "It's almost two-thirty."

"We're no match for real-life murderers," Ashley said. "I'm going to call my mother."

It was a good idea, but we had one small problem: not one of us had seen or heard a phone all week. "There must be one," Ashley insisted. "Nobody lives without a phone."

Abigail was in the kitchen. Ashley marched in and came right to the point. "Where's the phone?"

She frowned at us and asked, "Who do you want to call?"

"My mother. I have something important to tell her."

"You won't be able to reach her," Abigail said. "It's the last day of the conference and they said they wouldn't be back until very late. Is there a problem?"

That stopped us, but just for a minute. "But where's the phone anyway?" I asked. "I mean, just in case we ever had to make a call or something." I figured we could call the police.

"We keep it out of sight," Abigail said. "Tourists have a bad habit of running up big bills. If you need something, come to me. There aren't many problems that I can't solve."

Chapter

TWENTY-ONE

What are we going to do now?" Ashley asked. We were sitting in the living room, trying to come up with some answers. A light rain was falling; the day was dark.

"What *are* we going to do?" Ashley was pacing and wringing her hands, looking like some desperate heroine in an old movie.

"Quit asking that same question, Ashley," Peter said. "Why don't you use that brain of yours and think of something?"

Ashley stopped talking, stopped pacing, stopped wringing her hands. She plunked herself down in the middle of the floor, Indian style, and closed her eyes. She looked like she was going into a trance, and if I hadn't been so worried, I would have laughed.

All of a sudden her eyes snapped open and she bounced to her feet. "I've got it," she squealed. "I've got the answer," and she twirled around the room. "I'm brilliant. Stupendous. A genius."

"Calm down, Ashley," I said. "I can't think."

"That's the whole point," she said, still bouncing. "You don't have to think. I did it for you."

She sat down, looked around dramatically to make sure no one was around, and said, "Here's the deal. We know that Killeran and Albert are in on this together, right?"

"Right."

"And we also know that they're planning to use that dynamite tonight, right?"

"Right."

"And since Killeran is younger and probably smarter than Albert, he must be the ringleader. Right?"

"Okay, right."

"That means that without Killeran, Albert can't operate. So all we have to do is make sure we stick close to Killeran tonight. If we're around, he won't be able to do anything. Then tomorrow we'll tell Mom the whole story and she'll call the police."

I thought it over for a minute. "I guess so. But how do we manage to stick close to Killeran?"

She looked at me and frowned. "You can't expect me to think of everything, can you?"

"I know," Peter said. "Let's go to Killeran's for supper. We keep him busy; hang around until real late. They'll have to postpone their plans until another night. By then, the police will know the whole story and *bingo* that's the end of the plot."

"Fine," I said. "And how do you suggest we go to Killeran's for dinner? I don't think the sisters will let us."

We sat quietly thinking about this problem when Abigail walked into the room. "A storm is brewing," she said.

"Yeah," I said, thinking fast. "And we wanted to work on a National Seashore project for school. Mr. Killeran said he'd help us, but we have to go home tomorrow."

Peter picked up on my idea. "Too bad we couldn't have dinner with him and maybe spend the evening. But I guess that wouldn't be possible, would it?"

Abigail suddenly got more friendly than she had been all week. "I don't see why not," she said. "Your mothers won't be back until late, and with weather like this, we'll all be going to bed extra early. It might be nice for you to spend some time with Mr. Killeran. I'll even make something for you to take to him."

"Don't you think we should check with him first?" Peter asked.

"No need," was her quick reply. "It would be much more fun to surprise him. The man is lonely and he'd love to have supper with the three of you—I just know it." And she bustled out of the room, leaving the three of us staring at the door with our mouths open.

"You sure that was Abigail?" Peter asked.

"Maybe she put something extra in her soup at lunch," I said and laughed.

Ashley smiled. "Everything's working out perfectly."

By five o'clock the storm had gotten worse. A cold stinging rain beat on the windows and the fog made it look more like midnight than afternoon. I was sure Abigail would change her mind, but she came into the living room where we were finishing up the lighthouse puzzle and said, "You youngsters had better get ready. I've made a big pot of soup, and Albert will be here any minute to give you a ride over to Mr. Killeran's."

"Albert?" Ashley asked.

"I told him to give you a ride," she said.

That was typical of bossy old Abigail. She could even get someone who wanted to murder her to follow orders.

We went upstairs to get ready to leave. I made sure I still had the old pictures and revenge letter we had found in the attic as well as the xeroxed newspaper clipping I had taken from Killeran's. I wanted to make sure I didn't lose them, and I felt safest when they were with me.

We all squooshed into the front of Albert's truck. He grunted a little, but didn't talk on the ride over. When we got to Killeran's cottage, we piled out and I said, "Thanks for the ride. Maybe you'd better wait to see if he's—" but Albert drove off into the fog before I had a chance to finish.

"Does it strike you that something's not quite right?" I asked.

"I think Albert's mad because we're at Killeran's," Peter said. "Come on, hurry up. I'm getting wet."

Ashley was carrying a large notebook, a clipboard, extra paper, and five sharpened pencils. She figured we had to look like students. I was carrying the big pot of soup. Peter knocked on the door.

When Killeran saw the three of us, he looked like he was looking at three ghosts. "What . . . how . . . where did *you* come from?" he stuttered.

"Hi," Ashley said, putting on a big phony smile. "We thought we'd drop in for more information on the Seashore. We brought supper," and she wormed her way past him and into the cottage. We squeezed in right behind her.

Ashley kept talking. "I'm *so* interested in your job. And I'd be *so* excited to hear all about the National Seashore. It's *so* wonderful that you're *so* informed—" Killeran was looking madder and madder with each word. I was beginning to wonder if this was such a good idea. Peter cut her off and said, "We'd just appreciate a little of your time, Mr. Killeran."

Killeran shook his head slowly. "I know I told you to come back sometime, but I don't think . . ." His voice trailed off as he saw our looks of disappointment.

He looked at his watch. "I guess it'll be all right. But not for too long. I have some important work to do on the project. I'll drop you off right after dinner." He took the pot and headed for the kitchen.

"I hope we didn't make a mistake. He could be dangerous," I said. "Maybe we should have put sleeping pills or something in the soup."

"Not a good idea," Peter whispered. "We have to eat the soup, too."

"Oh, yuck! I forgot," I said, feeling my stomach turn.

"We'll have to keep on our guard, and keep him busy," Peter whispered.

"Maybe if we get him talking, he'll forget about the time," I suggested.

"Or maybe I'll have to pull a fainting spell," said Ashley, and she put the back of her hand to her forehead.

"Let's just hope we get out of this alive," I said.

TWENTY-TWO

"**A**nd last year over five million people visited the Cape Cod National Seashore.'' Killeran's voice droned on as the wind and rain howled around the cottage. I had the feeling he had given this same lecture a hundred times before. Killeran wasn't planning to kill us; he was going to bore us to death.

Killeran was finishing his third bowl of soup. I was still working on my first, trying to push aside the strange lumps and eat only the stuff I recognized, like carrots and potatoes.

Suddenly Killeran looked at his watch and said, ''I hate to eat and run, but I have to go. I'll drop you all back at the inn.''

''But we can't leave the dirty dishes on the table,'' Ashley said. ''We'll help you clean up.''

''Good idea,'' I said, starting to stack dishes. If Mom saw me, she'd be shocked. I never volunteered to do dishes at home.

We stalled as much as we could, but a half-hour later we were done and Killeran was ready to go.

We felt defeated. We were about to walk out the door when Ashley turned to me and asked, "Murphy, do you still have those old pictures?"

"Which ones?"

"The ones we found at the inn?"

"Yeah, they're in my pocket, but what do you—"

"Give me the one with the lighthouse," she said. I did. She turned to Killeran, who was halfway out the door, and said, "Mr. Killeran, do you have any old pictures of the Cape? Like this one? That we could use in our report? It would lend a real sense of history to it." And she handed him the picture.

He was obviously getting impatient with us. He looked at his watch, then glanced at the picture. "Sorry, I don't have any . . . Well, will you look at this. Where did you get this picture?"

"At the inn," Ashley said. "We found it."

Killeran took the picture over to the kitchen table and sat down. "Well, I'll be," he said. "It's one of the sisters."

We looked at each other—shocked. "What did you say?" Ashley asked.

But he didn't answer. He was too involved in looking at the picture.

Ashley whispered softly to both of us, "Either he's been doing a lot of snooping, or Albert's been talking."

Killeran was mumbling ". . . an old picture of one of the sisters." He turned it over and looked at the writing on the back. "The Beacon—I thought so."

"You know the sisters that well?" Peter asked.

"I've spent more time studying their history than anyone I know. We're like old friends."

"Sure you are," Ashley said in a nasty tone. Peter gave her a quick elbow.

"She's weathered pretty well, don't you think?" Killeran said. "She's a little worn now, but she's a proud old girl."

He jumped up. "And speaking of her, I really have to leave. Sorry. I've enjoyed the visit. Maybe you can come again." He started for the door. "The storm is getting worse. I'd better get you back to the inn."

"I have a lot more questions, Mr. Killeran," Ashley said quickly. "Couldn't you give us just a little more time? Please?" she whined.

"I'm sorry. I'd love to. But I can't. I'm late now, and I hate to keep people waiting."

Ashley changed her whine to anger. "It's just because we're kids. You're like all adults. You don't take us seriously."

He looked genuinely sorry. "I'd love to stay. But I'm worried about our latest project. Those old lighthouses we're working on are the only surviving triple lights in the country, and I'm scared to death that something's going to happen to them. You've seen them, haven't you? Set back in a clearing on Cable Road?"

"No, we haven't," Ashley said. "We've been here only a few days. Why don't you tell us about them?"

"I can't. Not now, anyway. The Beacon just arrived, and full security won't be in place until Monday morning. With all that's been going on, I want to make sure nothing happens to the old girl."

I sucked in my breath. "The Beacon?"

"Yes. She's the last to arrive. The Twins have been here for a while." He picked up the picture from the table and pointed. "That's her. The Beacon."

We gathered around him. He wasn't pointing to the girl in the picture; he was pointing to the lighthouse.

"We have big plans for them," he said. "Here, look at this map," and he picked up a map with three X's on it, like the one we saw in Albert's cottage. "This is where we've decided to put them. It's a spot between the Inn of the Three Sisters and the sea. But Albert Stark's the only native who's shown any interest in the project. I showed him the map and he wanted to see where we're planning to store the Beacon until we get her restored. He's been a big help to us."

The three of us just stood there looking at him and at each other. How could we have been so stupid? He must have noticed how confused we looked because he asked, "What's the matter? Did I say something to upset you?"

I was the first to recover my voice. "The Three Sisters? You mean to say there are lighthouses called the Three Sisters?"

"They're a national treasure, and my claim to fame— I hope. They were nicknamed the Three Sisters because sailors said they looked like three women wearing bonnets when they were built in 1892. Two of the lighthouses—the Twins—were sold at an auction in 1918. A woman named Mrs. Cummings paid $3.50 for both of them. Their lanterns were taken off and they became part of a cottage. The third lighthouse was sold years later when the government put up a new one. But she kept her lantern, so she's nicknamed the Beacon. That lantern is the only one of its kind that the government owns. Anyway, the government bought them back and I'm in charge of restoring them. We want them to look just like they used to. But some of the people around

107

here have given us a hard time. They're afraid that the lighthouses would be too much of a tourist attraction—and that means traffic and litter and noise—but there's nothing more historic than—"

Peter interrupted him. "They're going to get blown up. Tonight."

Killeran stopped talking and looked at him. "What are you talking about?"

"The Sisters. Someone wants to destroy them. Albert Stark, I think," said Peter.

"What makes you think that?"

We told Killeran about our trip to the old cottage, about the note we found and lost, about the figures disappearing into the graveyard tunnel, about the lights on the beach.

". . . and we saw dynamite in Albert's cottage. He's going to use it on the Sisters," I said. "We thought that Abigail, Bernice, and Cecily were in danger."

Peter's eyes brightened. "The sisters—the real ones, I mean. I'll bet you anything that they're in on it." He looked at Killeran. "We thought you hated them enough to want to 'eliminate' them."

"Me?" Killeran laughed. "They get on my nerves. But I'm not exactly a killer."

Everything was starting to fall together. "I'll bet that's why Abigail told us that mooncusser story the first night we were here. That way, if we saw anything—like those lights at night—we'd think it was our imaginations."

"And no wonder Abigail was so willing to let us come over here," Ashley said. "She figured we'd keep Mr. Killeran occupied and get rid of us at the same time."

"But what about those funny half-star symbols we

saw on the maps. What do they mean?'' I asked, and I drew Killeran a picture of the symbol.

"Oh, that's just a symbol for a lighthouse. It's a quick way for us to identify different types of buildings."

"Now I see it," said Peter. "The bottom half is the lighthouse, and the top part is the light."

"Let's get back to what you told me," Killeran said. "Someone's going to use dynamite on the Sisters?"

"Yes. Tonight," Peter said. "At least everything we've found and heard the last few days makes us think so."

"Then I'd better get moving. I don't know if you're right or not, but I don't want to take any chances. Come on, I'll drop you at the inn."

Chapter

TWENTY-THREE

As he headed for the door, the wind rattled the window panes and howled down the chimney. The lights flickered for an instant, then everything went black.

Killeran shuffled around for a minute, then switched on a flashlight. "This is bad," he said. "I had floodlights installed around the lighthouses to discourage vandalism, but with the power out, anything could happen."

"Take us with you," said Ashley. "If there are no lights and if the sisters are with Albert trying to blow up the lighthouses, we'll be all alone in the dark."

"But it's too dangerous," said Killeran.

"We'll stay in the truck," Peter suggested. "Away from danger."

Killeran hesitated a second and then said, "It's against my better judgment, but I also don't want to leave you at a dark, empty house. We'll take the jeep. But promise me you'll stay in it."

"We promise," the three of us said.

He went to a closet and pulled out some dark green ponchos. "You'd better put these on. They'll be a little big, but that storm is getting nasty."

We plopped the ponchos over our heads, went out into the storm, and piled into the jeep. With all the fog and rain, Killeran had to drive slowly. It seemed to take forever, but finally he pulled into a dirt road that opened into a wide clearing. The headlights of the jeep outlined three short, round buildings, two with no tops and one with a lantern still on it, and I recognized the shape of the lighthouses from the old picture.

I saw lights flickering around the lighthouses. Now and then weird shadows were thrown against the buildings by someone moving across the path of the headlights.

"Stay here," Killeran said. "We've had problems before with some people running around dressed in old clothes carrying lanterns. I think they've been trying to scare us, wanting us to believe the lighthouses were haunted."

Killeran headed for the lighthouses.

"Come on," Peter said. "Maybe we can help."

I expected Ashley to argue, but she was right with us. We didn't know where Killeran had gone, but the figure of a man, dressed in raggedy clothes and carrying a lantern, was going behind one of the lighthouses. It looked like he had sticks of dynamite in his other hand.

"Let's spread out," Peter called, and started running toward one of the lighthouses.

"Good idea," Ashley called back, and ran toward another.

I was about to head toward the third one when I felt a hand on my shoulder. I turned around, expecting to see Killeran, and came face to face with Abigail, dressed in the old-fashioned clothes we had seen in the cabin in the woods. She brought the lantern she was carrying close to my face and gasped. "What are *you* doing here?"

"Trying to help Mr. Killeran save the lighthouses. Why are you all doing this?" I shouted over the wind.

"Never mind," she shouted back. "Where are your friends?"

Before I could answer, three more ghostly figures came up beside her—Albert, Bernice, and Cecily—all dressed like old mooncussers and carrying lanterns. "The explosives are set," Albert said. "They must have been old. I had a hard time getting the fuses lit." He looked at me. "What's he doing here?"

I felt panic hit. "My friends are near those lighthouses somewhere," I hollered. "And so is Mr. Killeran."

They stood there looking at me. Cecily finally said, "I knew this would come to no good. I told you. Oh, those poor children." And she ran off toward the lighthouses.

"Cecily, come back," Abigail shouted. She looked at me. "We didn't want anyone to get hurt. We just didn't want the lighthouses to attract a lot of tourists. We knew no one was around guarding them now. But we have to save the children." And Albert, Bernice, and Abigail ran after Cecily.

I didn't know what to do, but I knew I had to look for Peter and Ashley. I ran toward the back of the left lighthouse, hoping to find the door, but once I was away from the jeep's headlights, it was pitch black. I stopped running. The blackness seemed to surround me, to close in on me.

And then, before I realized what had happened, the

dark clouds separated and a full moon threw its light over everything. I looked around and saw Albert running toward me.

"I planted two sticks in here," he said. "They've got very long fuses, but we have to hurry."

As we were about to go in, Peter was coming out. "I'm glad the moon came out," he said. "I was getting confused in the dark. Something's sputtering in there. I think we'd better get out of here."

We ran back toward the jeep. The three sisters were standing in a huddle.

"Where's Ashley?" I asked. "And Mr. Killeran?"

"The ranger went in there to find her," Abigail said, pointing toward the lighthouse on the right. "I hope it's not too late. We planted dynamite in all three of them."

The moon was still out, casting a glow over the whole scene. The rain was down to a drizzle, and I could feel myself shivering. I didn't know if it was because of the cold or fear. We waited—and watched.

Finally, Killeran came out of the lighthouse carrying Ashley. And Ashley was carrying a stick of dynamite at arm's length that was still sputtering.

"Throw it, Ashley," I shouted as they came closer. I had visions of all of us getting blown up.

Killeran set Ashley down. "She twisted her ankle on the old iron stairs. It's probably a slight sprain."

He was talking so calmly, I wanted to scream. I looked wide-eyed at the stick of dynamite as Killeran took it from Ashley, put it on the ground, and stepped on the fuse.

Albert looked at Killeran. "You don't understand," he said. "We planted two sticks in each of the light-

113

houses. Any second now, they're going to get blown to kingdom come—and us along with them."

Killeran picked up the stick his foot had snuffed out. "Where did you get these?" he asked. "They look like something from a shipment we received recently."

"From around here," Albert said. "They were in a box marked danger. We borrowed a few sticks. We thought it only proper to use government dynamite to get rid of the Sisters. We hated to do it, but it was the only way left to eliminate all the danged tourists they'd bring in."

Killeran laughed. "That's fine, Albert. But the next time you and the sisters plan to blow something up, make sure it's dynamite you're using and not flares."

Albert sucked in his breath. "What are you saying?"

Ashley was the one to answer. "These are flares, Albert. They look just like old sticks of dynamite, but they're not. Mr. Killeran told me that when he found me sitting next to one, crying and waiting to get blown up."

The moonlight let me see the expressions on all of their faces: Cecily was grinning, Bernice was smiling, Abigail looked relieved, and Albert looked confused. Then a cloud closed over the moon and it got dark again, except for the light from the jeep.

"Let's go back to the inn," Killeran said. "We have to get these kids into dry clothes and some ice on Ashley's ankle."

Chapter

TWENTY-FOUR

We first read about the plans for the lighthouses in the paper," Abigail was explaining as she set steaming mugs of cocoa in front of us. "They'd be right between us and the ocean, and that was okay because the inn was named for them. But then we found out there would also be a parking lot and tours and an information stand. And we thought about all the cars and buses and tourists and noise and litter. A lot of people got together and signed a petition and sent it to the government, but it didn't do any good. So we thought we could stop the project by scaring the workmen, and when that didn't work, we got the dynamite idea. I don't know—I guess we just got carried away."

"And I guess I didn't pay enough attention to how strongly you all felt about this," Killeran said. "I did get the petition, but I put it aside. I got so caught up in my project and felt so much pressure about money and deadlines. I'm sorry. There has to be a location for the lighthouses that will keep everyone happy."

"What about the sisters and Albert? Will they get into trouble?" I asked.

"No," Killeran said. "There's no law against lighting flares." He chuckled.

"And what about our house?" Abigail asked. "If you make it into a museum, where would we go?"

Killeran looked around. "It's a great old house—full of historic value. There are even rumors of underground tunnels that pirates used."

"That's no rumor," I said. "One of them starts in the jelly pantry and ends up in the old cemetery."

Abigail looked at me, smiled, and shook her head. "Leave it to youngsters to find the answers to everything. That's why I loved teaching school—the young ones were smarter than adults in lots of ways."

She sat down next to me and sipped her cocoa. "The tunnel was built years ago by our ancestors. They used it to bring in cargo they found on the beach—but they weren't really mooncussers, at least not as far as we know. We used it as a way to get in and out of the house when we didn't want our guests to know where we were. It was a way to keep tourists out of our business. When we had guests we wanted to get away from, we used a cabin in the woods that Albert owns. No one knows it's there."

When I started smiling, Abigail added, "Unless you young ones found that, too, somehow." It wasn't really a question, so I didn't feel I had to tell her.

Killeran, who had been listening closely, said, "There might be a way to keep everyone happy. The government has a land acquisition program—money to buy historic dwellings and lease them back to their owners, provided you keep the place in good repair and don't turn it into a motel or anything. We'd pay you a good price, and you could live in it for as long as you want."

Abigail thought for a minute. "Then we'd have enough money to live here without having to rent it out. It's not a bad idea. But I must admit, we do rent to some interesting people," and she smiled at us.

"But what about this?" I asked, pulling the threatening letter out of my pocket. "You wrote this, didn't you, Albert? About getting revenge?"

Albert took the letter from me and read it. "I guess I did," he said. Then, handing the letter to Cecily, he added, "And you know why."

Cecily flushed slightly. "A long, long time ago Albert fell in love with me, and I thought I loved him. But in those days I loved everyone—I had a new boyfriend every other week. Then Albert fell in love with Bernice and I guess I was a little jealous."

Cecily stood up as she talked, and it was like watching a great actress on the stage. "I would dress in Bernice's clothes and pretend to be her. I'd meet Albert and say terrible things to him. It was such fun fooling him, but I guess I got carried away. He got so mad he sent that awful letter. But by the time he figured out what was going on, Bernice had gone away. Albert left for a while, too. Then he came back and lived next door."

"I didn't know you kept that letter," Albert said quietly to Bernice.

"She kept all your other letters, too," Ashley blurted out.

117

Bernice dropped her eyes and Albert didn't look so mean anymore.

Ashley, sitting on the couch with her ankle propped up and iced, said, "Just like the movies."

"No," said Peter. "If there's one thing I learned this week, life is *not* like the movies."

As we packed the station wagon to leave the next morning, all three sisters gathered outside. "I hope the children weren't too much trouble," Mrs. Douglas said, as she gave Abigail a check for the week.

"Not at all," Abigail said. Peter and I shook hands with all three of them and thanked them for everything. Ashley, tears in her eyes, hugged Cecily and then Bernice. Then she went over to Abigail, who put her arms around Ashley and said, "You're a smart one, you are." She looked at Peter and me. "All of you. Smart as whips."

We piled into the station wagon. A smell drifted all around us—familiar somehow, but I couldn't place it.

I sniffed a few times. "Mom, what's that funny smell?" I finally asked.

She turned around and looked at us. "It's a surprise, or at least it's supposed to be. Abigail told us how much you loved her soup, so she gave us a big container to take home. And guess what? We talked her into giving us her secret recipe, so we can make her soup at home. It'll be a wonderful reminder of your vacation."

"Yeah," I groaned. "Wonderful!" And Peter and Ashley and I began to laugh.

As we started down the long, sandy driveway, I looked out the window at the fog that was beginning to drift in from the ocean. Suddenly, on the beach, I saw lights begin to flicker and sway, and I heard what sounded like an old horse neighing.

I looked back and saw Abigail, Bernice, and Cecily waving good-bye. I nudged Peter and pointed toward the beach. But the lights were gone.

About the Author

M. M. RAGZ is the writing coordinator for Stamford High School in Stamford, Connecticut. She literally does her writing on the run, developing story ideas while jogging five miles a day. While her job with the school system keeps her busy teaching writing, conducting writing workshops and seminars, and giving book talks, Mrs. Ragz occupies her free time with a range of activities that includes watercolor painting, crafts, gardening, and summers on Cape Cod in Eastham. She holds three college degrees from the University of Connecticut and Fairfield University. She has traveled to Germany, Mexico, Greece, Britain, and the Caribbean.

She lives in Trumbull, Connecticut, with her husband, Phil, and their youngest son, Michael, who is the inspiration for many of Murphy's adventures. Her other books about Murphy, *Eyeballs for Breakfast* and *Stiff Competition,* are available from Minstrel Books.